Sincerely Not Yours

BRITTNEY JOY

Brittney Joy/Horse Girl LLC

www.brittneyjoybooks.com

Publisher's Note: This is a work of fiction. Names, characters, places, and incidents are a product of the author's imagination. Locales and public names are sometimes used for atmospheric purposes. Any resemblance to actual people, living or dead, or to businesses, companies, events, institutions, or locales is completely coincidental.

Sincerely Not Yours / Brittney Joy; Horse Girl LLC --1st ed.

ebook ISBN: 978-1-958178-18-8

paperback ISBN: 978-1-958178-19-5

Newsletter Invitation

Never miss a new release ~ Sign-up for Brittney Joy's newsletter:

http://www.brittneyjoybooks.com/newsletter

Contents

For Stephanie,
You're my soul-sister. Thank you for your endless support, love &
laughter. Your friendship inspires the strong, loyal, loving friend-
ships I write. I'm beyond blessed to have you in my life.

Chapter One

Gigi Ricci's phone chimed, slicing through the early morning darkness and jerking her from a complicated dream, in which she'd lost all her teeth while also running late to high school math class. Sitting straight up in bed, she clutched the covers and gasped. Her hand went straight to her mouth. Confirming all her teeth were still present and accounted for, she slumped back into her pillows, releasing a breath.

It'd been nearly two decades since high school. Why did her sleeping brain torture her so? Couldn't she dream about tropical beaches with margaritas and handsome lifeguards? Or kittens and rainbows?

Still dazed, she squinted at the alarm clock. 5:56 a.m. blinked back at her in an accusation.

Who's texting me at this hour?

With a grunt, Gigi grabbed her phone from the nightstand. She swiped the notification and discovered a text from her boss. "Emergency meeting. Eight o'clock sharp. East conference room. Don't be late."

"That is *not* good," she mutter-whispered, but the message woke her as quickly as a shot of caffeine. Kim, her boss, was wound tight, but she didn't call emergency meetings unless there was a true disaster.

In record time, Gigi showered and threw herself together. She laced on tennis shoes and tossed a pair of dressy ballet flats into her tote bag, along with a thermos of coffee. Finally, she pulled on her peacoat and grabbed a container of yogurt to eat on the way to the office. Then she hit the streets of Chicago in a power walk. Her apartment was only eight blocks from work, but the last-minute meeting had her in a time crunch. She had a report due this morning that she hadn't quite finished last night. Now she'd have to complete it before Kim's meeting.

Fighting off the biting wind, she tugged her knit cap down to cover her ears before popping open her yogurt cup. With a plastic spoon, Gigi ate her breakfast and navigated the familiar route past tall stoic buildings on a quiet sidewalk covered with a light dusting of snow. Thankfully, there were few commuters to battle as she raced along, wondering what had blown up at the office.

Had they reduced next year's marketing budget? Were there issues with the Christmas ad campaigns or holiday product lineup? As the marketing director of SheTime, a Ryan & Ryan brand of premium beauty products, Gigi often navigated challenges, but the next few weeks were filled with holiday events. She didn't have time for a major crisis.

"Please don't let this be as bad as the apple pie-scented face-lotion fiasco." Her stomach squeezed as she recalled the same time last winter, which had also required an emergency meeting.

Last year, SheTime's fall beauty collection had a dessert theme, and the bestselling fragrance was "spiced apple pie." However, a last-minute change to one of the antiaging ingredients in the face lotion had caused a strange reaction with the fragrance. After applying it, the sweet scent turned sour and smelled more like stinky feet than spiced apple pie.

Gigi groaned, pushing through the revolving door and into the office lobby. The social media backlash had been brutal, and it'd been Gigi's responsibility to clean up the mess. A true PR nightmare.

Because no one wanted their face to smell like stinky feet. *Obviously.*

With a wave to the security guard, Gigi strode through the quiet lobby, hoping the emergency meeting was good news, like an early Christmas bonus or a larger marketing budget for the next year. Maybe an assistant? Something that would make her smile rather than scream. Scraping the bottom of the yogurt container, Gigi wished she knew what the meeting was about and considered texting her boss, but got distracted by the closing elevator door ahead.

"Hold the door, please!" she called, breaking into a jog. The office was in a historic building, making it an architectural gem with ornate stone archways and marble floors. That also meant the elevators were notoriously slow. She didn't have a minute to spare this morning.

Miraculously, a large, masculine hand appeared, catching the door and pushing it open.

"Thanks," Gigi sighed, slipping inside to discover a man standing near the control panel.

"Good Morning. What floor?" Dressed impeccably in a tailored charcoal-gray suit, he greeted her with an indifferent nod. The fabric clung to his tall frame, accentuating a lean, muscular silhouette. Everything about him was meticulous. Polished. Expensive. His piercing green eyes sized her up in a way that gave her the jitters.

"Morning," she replied, but as the door squeezed shut, Gigi squirmed. She was suddenly conscious of her own appearance. Warm from the hurried walk, she'd opened her peacoat, exposing jeans and a cat-themed sweater. And it wasn't just any cat-themed sweater. It was green and red, with three felines sporting tiny scarves and hats. Around the cats, there was embroidery that proclaimed *Meowy Christmas*. If she was being honest, it was one of her favorite sweaters. It just seemed a little out of place next to the suit guy. Besides the sweater, she had pulled her knit hat so low that it nearly covered her eyes. And to top off her too-early-for-this ensemble, Gigi held a yogurt cup in one hand and a plastic spoon in the other—which contained her last bite of yogurt.

She must look like a crazy person who'd wandered in off the streets.

"I work here," she blurted, not able to control the urge to justify herself to this stranger. One of her tennis shoes was untied, and she almost informed the man that she'd packed ballet flats to change into. Of course, she'd run into Mr. Tall, Dark, and Handsome the day she looked like a jigsaw puzzle with a couple of missing pieces.

He arched a well-groomed brow. "I believe you." Though he didn't sound like he did. "What floor?" He pointed to the control panel, reminding her of his unanswered question.

"Four, please." Gigi analyzed his dark hair as he hit the button. Had he intentionally styled it to look perfectly mussed? When he pressed the tenth-floor button for himself, she straightened, as that was where the top of SheTime's corporate ladder resided. Maybe he was a banker or investor? One of Mr. Ryan's tennis club friends? Though they usually showed up at the office in expensive athleisure wear—not tailored suits.

"Casual Friday?" the man asked as the elevator rose. She scrunched her brow, bristling at his critical undertone, but tampered a sarcastic reply. Probably not in her best interest to lip off to anyone on their way to the tenth floor.

"Actually, it's Football Friday." She gave him a closed-lip smile. *You're going to be drastically overdressed for your meeting.*

He peered at her out of the corner of his eye. "Football Friday?"

Gigi pushed her hat up and out of her eyes. "Yes. It's like casual Friday, except with jerseys. The Ryans are big football fans. They'll be wearing Bears jerseys and jeans, if you're meeting with them today." She scanned his face for confirmation. He didn't give it to her. Instead, Mr. Swanky Suit clasped his hands in front of him, looking curious.

"But no football jersey for you?"

She shook her head. "Not a fan. Can't get interested in a game where men pile on top of one another and compete for the most traumatic brain injury." Gigi shrugged, not understanding the diehard passion people felt for the game. It bored her to pieces. "But, to each their own. No offense if you enjoy football."

His eyebrows rose, but a hint of amusement played on his lips. "No offense taken."

"Good," she chirped.

A beat passed before the man asked, "But why the cat sweater?"

It was a valid question. She still quirked a brow at him. "Just because I don't like football doesn't mean I can't take part in a day meant to celebrate something I love. Instead of sports gear, I always wear a sweater showcasing something I actually enjoy." She cleared her throat. "Cats. Christmas. Knitting. I have another sweater with tiny margaritas and limes."

Her comment instigated a crooked grin from the stranger—one that sent Gigi's heart skipping out of rhythm. Gosh dang, he was handsome. In a classical, grouchy, stiff kind of way. Her stomach dipped in contrast to the rising elevator, and she immediately distracted herself by searching through her tote bag for her phone.

You have the worst taste in men, Gigi reminded herself. If butterflies were swarming her belly, he likely had a wife at home, a mistress, or a gambling problem. Or all three. He also could've just escaped from jail. Those were the type of men she was drawn to—ones that covered major flaws with a chiseled jaw and a boatload of charisma.

The elevator dinged, stopping at the fourth floor. Gigi located her phone and pulled it from the bottom of her bag.

"Have a great day." She waved, stepping toward the opening door and recalling the pact she'd made with herself—no more dating. Not for a while . . . or maybe ever. The yo-yo of emotions it brought was more than her heart could handle. She was much better off focusing on work and friends.

The man tipped forward to hold the door open for her. She turned to say a simple "thank you," but the words never left her mouth. They got stuck in her throat when her gaze connected with his bright, sea-glass eyes. The intensity that lingered in an ocean of aqua and green momentarily ensnared her. And her stupid, slush-covered feet stumbled over the untied laces.

Gigi slid as though she were ice skating. And she'd never been good at any sport. Her feet flew in opposite directions and she became a mess of flailing limbs.

"Oh!" she yelped, trying to catch her balance as her phone shot out of her hand like a bullet, going God knows where. But that was the least of her worries. If she didn't get some traction, she'd end up in the splits.

Trying to help, the man lurched forward. He grabbed her arm, but she was mid-flail and accidentally smacked him in the face. The back of her hand hit his cheek. *Hard.*

"Oof," he groaned, skittering sideways and losing hold of her.

"Holy moly!" Gigi ran in place like Scooby-Doo for what seemed like forever before her legs tangled with the stranger's and they both tripped out the elevator door. As they tumbled, Gigi's forehead connected with his jaw like the smack of a hammer hitting a nail, which instigated expletives from them both.

Ugh . . .

Ouch!

They hit the floor, and then it was silent. Mainly because the man was flat on his back, and Gigi was on top of him, her face buried in his neck.

"Oh my God," she uttered, with the little breath left in her lungs. Her words were stifled, her lips pressed against warm skin. When she inhaled spicy aftershave, she peeled her face from his neck, not believing the predicament she'd gotten herself into. She was trying to walk away from a handsome temptation, and the universe had put her smack on top of him.

Gigi lifted her head. Not sure what to do, she put a hand on his shoulder and pushed up, placing her lips just inches from his. Suddenly, she couldn't breathe. Mainly because her Christmas kittens pressed against his abnormally hard chest. And abs.

Heat flushed her cheeks.

"I—" she started, wanting to apologize for slapping him in the face and then pulling him to the ground.

He moved his jaw like he wasn't sure if it was broken. "You sure you don't like football? That was one heck of a tackle."

So. Freaking. Embarrassing.

This guy was definitely going straight to Mr. Ryan's office to claim assault.

"I—" Gigi started again, meaning to apologize, but there were other, more distracting words echoing through the quiet hall.

When she lost her phone, she must've unlocked her screen and opened an app, because the device was on the ground, playing the audiobook Gigi had drifted off to the night before—a romance by her favorite author. To her horror, it had started in the middle of a vivid kissing scene. The narrator's husky voice echoed through the empty corridor, colorfully describing a passionate lip lock with throbbing hearts and pressing bodies.

Gigi gasped. Heat seared her face as the man's eyes went wide, and Gigi became extra aware of how she was draped over him.

Swearing, she jumped up, making the man grunt with her quick retreat. Her phone was a few strides away, and she sprinted for it, diving to silence the audiobook before another steamy word could leave the speaker. Then, in the deafening quiet, she looked over. The man was standing, brushing down the front of his suit. The look on his face was anything but amused.

A nervous laugh escaped her. "Audiobooks. That's another thing I love. Cats, knitting, margaritas, and audiobooks." She wanted to shrink into a ball and roll into the cubicles behind her.

Mr. Swanky Suit gave her a tight smile before pressing the elevator call button. "Interesting start to my day," he noted, and the door opened.

"Hope the rest of your day is better," she called with forced optimism. He nodded and disappeared. Quickly, Gigi gathered her tote bag and what was left of her dignity. Sighing, she headed for her desk, running a hand over her face in disgust.

Could she be any more of a mess this morning? She'd completely embarrassed herself in front of some guy on the way to meet with one of the Ryans. And now she'd probably also have a big goose egg on her forehead. Her only consoling thought was that, at the very least, she'd never see Mr. Swanky Suit again.

Chapter Two

"If Dad wants to sell the company, SheTime needs to be dissolved," Harris said, leaning against the cold window of his brother's corner office. His gaze drifted down to the gridlocked traffic far below. Cars jammed the streets, mirroring the irritation growing inside him.

"Harris, we've been over this. Dad's just trying to get you back into the business. He doesn't really want to sell." Dean, his younger brother and the current CEO of Ryan & Ryan, stood from his sleek mahogany desk. He stared at Harris in disbelief, though it was hard to take him seriously in his football jersey.

"Dad doesn't make empty threats."

"That's why I asked you to come back and talk some sense into him."

Harris pulled his hand from his pocket and ran it through his hair. "Once Dad makes up his mind, there's no talking sense into him. You know that as well as I do." Their dad was as stubborn as a mule, and he wasn't likely to change his mind about his most recent decision—to retire and pass on the family business to *both* of his sons.

"You seriously think Dad's going to retire and spend his days cruising the Bahamas? Or doing crossword puzzles?" Harris couldn't hide the snark in his questions. Their dad was not the average seventy-year-old. He didn't know the meaning of "relaxation." Never had. Harris couldn't picture him not working. He'd always meddle with the company, in some form. In fact, if it weren't for his new wife, their dad would continue working until death came knocking at his office door.

"Nah." Dean shook his head. "More like trips to Paris and Italy. Karen's already planned a month in Europe for her and Dad in the spring. And then they're going to spend the summer at the lake house. They want the grandkids to come visit them."

Harris nearly choked on his tongue. "Seriously?"

"Serious as a snowman in a heatwave." Dean rounded his desk and Harris squinted at him, not able to connect the father he knew with the husband Karen was hoping for. The only vacations Harris remembered from his childhood were before his mother had passed. His father would fly in to join them for a day or two. Or not at all.

Pressing the length of his arm against the window, Harris leaned into the chilled glass. "Didn't take her long to convince him to retire, huh?"

Dean furrowed his brow. "What do you mean? They've been married for seven years, and she's been bugging him to retire since the wedding."

"Seven years?" Had it really been that long?

"I think you'd actually like Karen if you took the time to get to know her. She's good to Dad and the kids love her."

Harris nodded, slowly. He didn't really have a reason not to like Karen. It was his dad he didn't trust. Karen was his fourth wife. He'd remarried a few years after Mom passed, and it'd taken Harris most of his teenage years to warm up to his stepmom. Then, after high-school—once she felt like family—his dad and she divorced and Harris lost another major part of his life. He married again for a few short years in his fifties. Even now, Harris didn't trust that his dad fully committed to much, at least outside of work.

"I'm sure she's nice. She's got to have the patience of a saint to put up with Dad," Harris said, and Dean shrugged in agreement. "But I'm not here to talk about Dad's marriage. I'm here to talk about the future of Ryan & Ryan." His shoulders squared, considering the ultimatum Dad had given them. "I've got my own life. I can't just drop everything because Dad decided it's time for me to play the dutiful son."

Dean sighed. Worry etched his face. Their dad wanted *both* his sons working for the family business. If that didn't happen, he'd sell Ryan & Ryan next year to their largest competitor, a billion-dollar conglomerate that'd turn and burn the business. That was why Harris was here, standing in Dean's office and placating their father.

Though he wasn't here for their father. He was here for Dean.

"I get it," Dean said. "I really do. But it's not just about the company, Harris. It's about us. We're a family. We built this together. I don't want to lose the company Grandpa started with blood, sweat, and tears. Do you?"

The brothers locked eyes, the weight of family history and expectations hanging in the air.

"Grandpa is rolling over in his grave right now, Dean. He'd smack Dad upside the head for even considering the situation he's put us both in." Harris shook his head. His brother wanted to take over the family business. It was all he'd ever wanted since they were little. Harris was content to live the life he'd created for himself in New York City. But their dad had thrown a wrench into both of their plans, mainly because it irked him that Harris had made his own way. He had his own thriving business, making it hard for his dad to control him.

"I'm here for you." Harris fixed his stare on Dean. "I'll stay through Christmas. Hopefully, we can persuade Dad to sell to you by then." Even if it forced Harris to work alongside his dad, something he swore he'd never do again. But if they couldn't change their dad's mind by Christmas, Harris was certain his mind would never change.

Dean's shoulders sagged in obvious relief, and he gave Harris a crooked smile. "Thanks for coming, brother."

Harris nodded. He stood from the window, rubbing a hand over his jaw in thought, but a throb of pain reminded him of the headbutt he'd received this morning—from a curiosity of a woman. Picturing her, Harris wondered what she did at Ryan & Ryan. She didn't fit the mold, and that intrigued Harris. Even now, he couldn't help grinning at her explanation of the cat sweater. Harris was sure it irked his father to no end. His dad loved football and needed everyone around him to fall in line with his way of thinking. Particularly if they were on his payroll.

Harris smirked, appreciating her tenacity. But when his mind wandered to her angelic face and the gentle curve of her lips—which he had studied when she had been draped on top of him—he cleared his throat and shifted to a new subject. The last thing he needed was to get distracted by a woman. Especially, one that worked for his father.

"I'm going to run a full analysis on SheTime," Harris announced. "I ran the financials last night, and that division is bleeding money." At least he could make himself useful while he was here.

"It's an investment in our future. There's a lot of marketing involved in growing a new brand."

Harris crooked an eyebrow. "What's wrong with the economical soaps we've been manufacturing for fifty years?"

"Nothing's wrong with them," Dean said. "They're the bread and butter of Ryan & Ryan, but we also need to change with the times. SheTime is a premium line for women. It's diversifying our business, and it's got a lot of potential."

Dean had always been a "big picture" kind of guy, while Harris focused on the details. He was analytical, making decisions based on sound data and financials. "I'm all about diversification, but only if it's profitable. From what I saw in the quarterly reports, SheTime's running on slim margins and has been for a while. Doesn't make sense to keep throwing money at a failing business. Dissolving that division would help the bottom line. Even if Dad ends up selling, it'd increase profitability and guarantee a better sale price."

Dean gave a quick shake of his head. "We can't just get rid of an entire division at the drop of a hat. Do you want me firing a bunch of people before Christmas?"

"When you put it like that, you make me sound like a complete grinch."

Dean stared at him, not arguing the grinch part.

Ouch.

"You don't have to fire everyone," Harris added. "I'm sure you could move some roles within the company."

"How about instead of dissolving SheTime, you help me *fix it*?" He put air quotes around the last two words, challenging Harris.

Harris slid a hand in his pocket. "I'll pull together a full financial analysis and recommendation by the end of the week. I already started with last quarter's—"

Dean held up a hand. "You need to understand the business outside of reports and spreadsheets."

Was there a more efficient way? Harris cocked his head. "What do you have in mind?"

"I want you to take over as SheTime's director." Dean looked way too excited for his own good. "While you're here," he added.

"Have you been sitting on that the entire time we've been talking?"

"Maybe."

Harris huffed. "Don't you already have a director?"

"She's leaving. Just put in her resignation. Pregnant with baby number three and wants to stay home with her kids."

"Well, that's inconvenient." Harris rubbed a temple with two fingers.

Dean laughed. "Inconvenient for who?"

"Me. You."

"Come on," Dean urged. "This way, you can learn the intricacies of that division's business. I'll let you do whatever you want in the next two weeks, and if by Christmas, you still think SheTime should be dissolved, then I'll take your recommendation."

Harris would rather learn from behind a computer, but liked the idea of making the calls for the next few weeks. And if interacting with the sales and marketing team was the only way to open Dean's eyes, he'd do it. From the numbers he'd seen, the team needed direction, anyhow. Besides, the annoyance would be short-lived. "Alright, but I'll need access to everything—financials, operations, marketing strategies."

Dean jerked his arm back like the Bears had finally made a touchdown. "You'll have it. Gigi, the marketing director, can brief you on her current projects."

"Gigi?" Harris raised an eyebrow, immediately associating "Gigi" with the slim margins he'd reviewed. She didn't focus on the right metrics and frivolously spent on extravagant packaging, advertising, and events, seriously cutting into profits.

"Yeah, she's been doing a great job. Smart. Creative. You'll be in good hands."

"Mm-hmm," Harris said, going along with his brother's positivity. Even though he didn't agree with it.

"Actually, I'll introduce you now. Kim called a meeting to tell the team about her resignation. They should still be in the conference room."

Harris had tougher topics to address with their father, but playing director would make it look like he was interested in diving back into the family business. That'd give him more leverage in their conversations.

Buttoning his suit coat, Harris nodded at Dean. "Alright. Let's get this over with."

Chapter Three

"I'm so excited for you," Gigi said to Kim, smiling through the panic rising inside her. "I just can't believe you're leaving."

"I know, I know." Kim sighed, handing Gigi her laptop like she was handing off a baton. "But working full time and raising two kids is driving me to insanity. I can't imagine what it's going to be like with three. I wish I could clone myself."

Gigi pursed her lips, trying to understand Kim's decision. "You sure you want to resign, though?" It was hard to picture Kim as a stay-at-home mom. She wasn't exactly the warm and fuzzy type.

"Yeah," Kim replied, though her face didn't exude confidence. She sighed again. "Last week, little Joseph called the nanny 'Mommy.' I missed Danny's first steps, and I can't even remember the last time I went on a date with my husband. Something is going to break if I don't make a change, and it might be me."

Gigi offered a sympathetic smile. "I get it. You need to put your family first."

"I'm sorry to spring this on you with the Gal's Gift Guide events just starting." Kim gave her a flat smile. "But I don't know how much help I'd be, anyhow. My morning sickness has been terrible with this one." She placed a hand on her stomach. "Actually, it's more like all-day sickness."

"It's okay. I can handle it," Gigi consoled Kim, noticing how pale she was. "It's not a problem." She brightened her expression, even as she wondered how she'd do it. Honestly, Gigi was practically at her breaking point herself. It wasn't like SheTime had a big team. Outside of Kim and Gigi, there was one product manager and two sales reps. They'd all given Kim their congratulations and were exiting the conference room, leaving empty coffee cups and a hard-hit box of donuts on the table near the door.

"I'm sure I can round up some help from the team," Gigi added, knowing their schedules were tight this time of year too. She had three weeks full of holiday events, all of which were outside of work hours. How was she going to do it by herself?

"You'll have help." Kim gave her a pat on the shoulder just as Dean walked through the door. "Dean and I already talked about it."

"Good morning," Dean greeted them with a big smile, but Gigi's attention fell on the tall man who followed behind him.

Is that . . . ? Her insides hiccupped.

Sharp gray suit. A jaw that could cut glass. Hypnotic, sea-glass eyes.

Mr. Swanky Suit?

"Gigi," Dean greeted. "I'd like to introduce you to my brother, Harris."

Gigi blinked. *Hard.* Did Dean say this was his brother?

For a moment, Harris's eyes went wide with recognition. Was this morning's disastrous encounter replaying through his head? Because all Gigi could think about was how she'd slapped, tripped, and head-butted this man, before landing on top of him while her spicy audiobook played in the background.

Oh. My. God.

Dean looked between Gigi and his brother. "Do . . . you guys know one another?" he asked, confused.

The surprise vanished from Harris's face. "We ran into each other this morning on the elevator." Gigi's stomach clenched, waiting for him to expand on how they ran into each other. Instead, he offered his hand. "But we didn't get properly introduced. I'm Harrison—Harris—Ryan."

"Oh," Gigi squeaked, shaking his hand absentmindedly as she connected the dots. "Pleasure to meet you, Mr. Ryan." She'd made a complete fool of herself with Harrison Ryan? The prodigal son who'd infamously left the family business? "Gianna Ricci." She gave her full first name, as if that would help repair his image of her.

Kim squinted at Gigi. "Do you prefer being called Gianna?"

No. Only her mother called her that—when she was mad.

Gigi shrugged noncommittally. "You can call me Gigi."

"Okay." Harris nodded, accepting her offer. "Nice to meet you, Gigi."

"Alrighty then," Dean said, dismissing the awkward introduction, seemingly unaware of the elevator mishap. "Kim already knows this, but Harris will be taking over for her."

Kim bobbled her head, looking content with this piece of information. Gigi was stunned. This past summer, when rumors had swirled through the office that Harrison Ryan might come back to the family business, she'd heard a million different reasons why he left. None of them were good. He'd run off with his secretary. He'd embezzled, stealing from his dad. He'd gone on a bender in Vegas.

She didn't trust this guy. Why was he back?

"You're taking over for Kim?" Gigi asked, remembering the other piece of gossip she'd heard. The "other Ryan brother"—the one staring at her like she was a mystery he needed to solve—had created that notorious dating app, GambleOnLove. It was wildly popular, but for all the wrong reasons. It was an app people used to hook up, not to find love.

This guy was going to run a business that catered to women? Did he even know what women wanted?

"Yes," Harris confirmed with a nod. "And I've already reviewed SheTime's financials. They're concerning. We need to make it more profitable. That'll be my priority."

Gigi's stomach sank like a rock in a river.

"More profitable?" she questioned, unable to hide the skepticism in her tone. Gigi had poured her heart into building this brand, and now the brother that'd abandoned his family and made a sketchy dating app was going to mess with it? She glanced at Dean, but he didn't look as worried as she felt. "How so?"

Harris tilted his head, emphasizing his arrogance. "By making smart business decisions. We need to align our investments with our business goals. We can't continue supporting a brand that isn't making money."

Gigi's cheeks flamed, but this time, it wasn't from embarrassment. Was he insinuating that SheTime was a poor investment? Anger bubbled in her chest, threatening to spew out.

Kim intervened, sensing the tension. "Gigi, Harris has a background in business and technology. I'm sure he'll bring valuable insights to SheTime. You two will make a great team."

Gigi pressed her lips together, keeping her skepticism and comments to herself.

"And speaking of teams," Kim continued, "Harris will help you with the Gal's Gift Guide events."

Gigi's eyes widened. She almost dropped the laptop she'd been clutching. "Wait, what?" She exchanged a quick glance with Harris, who seemed equally unenthusiastic about the idea.

"I don't know about that—" Harris started, but Dean jumped in, interrupting his brother.

"That's right." Dean smiled brightly, overcompensating for his brother's blatant rudeness. "Harris is going to take Kim's spot and attend the Christmas events with you."

"I don't know if that's a good idea." Harris spoke up, clearly not thrilled about the prospect. "Dean, I saw what these events are costing us. Why don't we focus on the bottom line and skip the holiday fluff? We don't need these events to sell soap to women."

Sell soap to women? Gig's mouth hinged open. SheTime was so much more than that. Clearly, this guy didn't have a clue about the business. And now he was going to be running it?

"Not happening." Her words came out sharp. Harris grimaced like she'd poked him with a pointy stick. "SheTime is a major sponsor of the Gal's Gift Guide. We've already committed. There's no backing out now. It starts tomorrow." She'd spent all year planning the event with the Chicago Women's Association, but Harris saunters in and suddenly knows best? He wanted to cut the event with no concept of the backlash? "If we cancel, we won't get reimbursed for our sponsorship. Plus, we'd lose out on the opportunity to connect with thousands of holiday shoppers, both at the events and through the extensive media campaigns." Not to mention, the company would look ridiculous for canceling last minute.

"See?" Dean shrugged, looking happy at Gigi's rebuttal. "No cost savings in canceling. Looks like you're going to be busy for the next few weeks."

"Few weeks?" Harris looked like he'd just seen the Ghost of Christmas Past. "How many of these events are there?"

"Ten," Gigi said, raising a brow.

"You've got to be joking," Harris replied.

"It's the perfect way for you to learn about the business," Dean said, still smiling despite Harris's furrowed brow and deep frown. "You'll have time to interact with customers and understand the product. It'll be your crash course for SheTime, and a lot more informative than just staring at spreadsheets." Dean locked gazes with Harris, and they seemed to exchange an entire conversation without another word.

Finally, Harris blew out a breath. "Fine," he conceded.

"Great!" Dean smacked his hands together in a clap. "You'll get to spend a ton of time with Gigi. She's very knowledgeable about the market. You could learn a lot from her." Dean gave Gigi a supportive smile.

Harris squinted, looking suspicious, but he didn't protest further.

"Great," Gigi replied, but without the same enthusiasm as Dean. She couldn't shake the bad feeling coursing through her. Kim was leaving and her new boss was about to rip apart all of Gigi's hard work. The Gal's Gift Guide would be a disaster. After all, what could the creator of a hookup-dating-app contribute to a business that catered to women? His values were about as far from SheTime's as one could get.

Working with him was like discovering a big lump of coal in her Christmas stocking.

Chapter Four

"He's the worst," Gigi declared to her friends, Alice and Paige. The three of them were cozied up in Alice's apartment for their weekly "Yappy Hour," which included margaritas, girl talk, and various other activities. They cooked together, watched movies, and did a lot of laughing. Tonight, they were knitting—a hobby Alice had recently picked up. As the crafter of the group, she was teaching Gigi and Paige, and Gigi found the rhythmic click of the needles oddly soothing. Paired with great conversation and drinks, it was the perfect antidote to a stressful week.

"He just walked in and started barking orders?" Alice's eyes were wide and unbelieving. She stared at Gigi from the armchair where she sat cross-legged, dressed in leggings and a cowlneck sweater.

Two needles moved swiftly in her hands, pulling from the bundle of yarn in her lap.

"Yeah," Gigi huffed and snuggled deeper into the couch's big pillow, leaving her needles and yarn splayed out on the cushion next to her. She had exactly two rows of stitches completed on a scarf she wanted to give to her sister for Christmas. Alice had helped her restart it three times. Instead of working on her gift, Gigi was petting Alice's husky black-and-white cat, Mister Tuxedo. He purred in her lap. "He made some flippant comment about SheTime not being profitable and said he was going to 'fix' that." She made air quotes, along with a disgusted face. "Then he stared me down with those grumpy, sea-glass eyes like I was the bane of his existence."

"Sea-glass eyes?" Paige piped up, showing interest in the one descriptor Gigi hadn't meant to divulge. "You conveniently *forgot* to tell us what Harris looks like. Is your new boss a hunk?" Paige had barely recovered from her giggle fit after Gigi had reenacted her encounter with Harris in the elevator. "So . . . what does he look like? Do tell." Paige was spread across the other armchair, her legs hanging over one armrest, a half-empty margarita glass in one hand. The salted rim was inches from her lips.

"He's not ugly," Gigi admitted, noncommittally. "But he'd be a lot cuter if he wasn't trying to blow up my life."

"Why didn't Dean promote you to director, in place of Kim?" Alice asked. "You've been running that division for years."

"Yeah, you seriously do it all. You could step right into Kim's role," Paige added.

Gigi smiled at her supportive friends. "Thanks, guys." The thought had crossed her mind as well. She would've jumped at the chance for the promotion, but wasn't given the option. "I guess I don't have the right last name."

"That's stupid." Paige sipped her drink and tucked her dark, curly hair behind an ear. "I guarantee you're more qualified than Harris. Even if it is his family's business."

"Why'd he come back suddenly?" Alice asked, quirking a brow.

"I'm not sure," Gigi said, recounting Harris's disapproving looks and all the rumors she'd heard. "But I think he's got something to prove." In the conference room, she could almost see a chip sitting on his shoulder.

"Like what?" Paige slid her legs off the armrest, sitting up curiously. She leaned forward, sipping her margarita while peering at Gigi over the rim. "You have some juicy gossip to share?"

The three of them shared everything. Nothing went outside of their circle—unless Paige put it in one of her books. But even then, names were changed, and Paige tweaked the information to fit her stories. Gigi loved reading Paige's books and finding Easter eggs that only she and Alice would catch.

Pursing her lips, Gigi considered her intel and then spewed it. "He's the oldest son. Used to work for his dad a decade ago, alongside Dean. Something happened. I'm not sure what, but I'm going to get to the bottom of it. He quit and ran off to New York City. Hasn't been back to the office until now."

"He hasn't been back for ten years?" The needles in Alice's hands moved faster, blazing through another row of the blanket she was knitting. She leaned forward, waiting for more information. "What's he been doing?"

Gigi quirked a brow, ready to clue her friends in on the next juicy tidbit. "You know that dating app, GambleOnLove?" She scratched Mister Tuxedo's head. He rolled around in her lap, purring louder.

"I've heard of it." Alice paused, tugging at one of her stitches. "I think."

"The one that's like Russian Roulette?" Paige cocked her head, using one of her knitting needles as a stir stick—which was how she preferred to use her needles. Ice clinked against the glass. "Isn't that the app that was all over the news when the governor used it to cheat on his wife?"

"Yep, that's it," Gigi confirmed, reaching for the saucy plate of meatballs on the coffee table and poking one with a toothpick. "Harris Ryan created it. He owns GambleOnLove." She popped the meatball in her mouth and chewed, feeling vindicated in her disapproval of her new boss.

"The app?" Paige gasped, halting her stirring. "He's got to be worth a fortune. That app blew up after it was all over the news."

Gigi licked sauce from her bottom lip, enjoying the spicy tang of the meatballs she'd whipped up last night. "I'm more concerned that the guy who created a hook-up app will now run SheTime. Obviously, he doesn't know what women want or need, and that's going to be a problem." She didn't care about his net worth. She cared that he was going to mess with her job.

Paige nodded slowly, considering Gigi's predicament. "That could definitely make your day-to-day interesting."

"Interesting? I was thinking more along the lines of painful." Gigi sighed, slumping back against the couch and running through all the ways Harris could upend all her hard work.

"How does the app work?" Alice asked, pulling her long, silky hair over a shoulder and out of her cowlneck. "It's been so long since I've been in the dating scene. All these apps are like a foreign language to me."

It didn't surprise Gigi that Alice wasn't familiar with GambleOnLove. She'd been dating her boyfriend for seven years and waiting on an engagement ring for the past six—which really irritated both Gigi and Paige. How could Alice's boyfriend *not* put a ring on it? She was an absolute catch. Total devoted-wifey material.

"I'm not exactly sure how it works." Gigi didn't know the details, except what she heard on the news. She stayed off dating apps. Even if she was looking for love, she'd much prefer finding it organically. Like at a farmer's market. Or a coffee shop. She didn't trust anyone hiding behind technology. "But I know it's anonymous. That's why the governor was using it. It's completely anonymous until you meet your match in person. No pictures or anything."

"What?" Alice asked, with a gasp. "So, you don't even get to see the person until you meet them?"

"Yep," Gigi confirmed.

Alice and Gigi wrinkled their noses at each other, disturbed by the concept, but Paige had other ideas. She grabbed her phone and started tapping away.

"Now you've got me curious." Paige focused on her phone. "I need to know how this app works. I'm downloading it now."

"What? No!" Gigi yelped, but she couldn't deny she was also curious. Especially since the creator was her new boss. She'd be spending a lot of time with him from now until Christmas.

"It's research. We're getting to the bottom of this," Paige declared, in her I'm-not-taking-no-for-an-answer voice. Gigi chuckled, knowing she couldn't stop her. Out of the group, Paige was the most daring. She enjoyed pushing boundaries, and Gigi admired her for it. Even if she thought it was a waste of time to research Harris's app.

As Paige set up the app, Gigi grabbed her needles and completed a few more stitches, though they didn't look anywhere near as neat as Alice's work. Hopefully, Gigi's sister wouldn't mind a scarf that looked like an abstract piece of art. She plucked at a loose stitch. At least it'd be warm.

"Okay, okay. Here's the gist of it." Paige held up a finger, getting everyone's attention. She scrolled. "You have to set up a profile, using your basic information, interests, location, and dating preferences, but the only public-facing information is your username."

Gigi set her needles on her lap, on top of Mister Tuxedo. "OMG! I just remembered the governor's username . . . it was Hanging-WithMyGnomies!"

"No!" Alice giggle-squeaked.

"Yes!" Gigi replied, before they all broke into belly laughs.

"That's so wrong and so funny!" Paige huffed and shook her head. Her eyes traveled back to her phone, scrolling to read more. "When you're ready to be matched, you spin a virtual wheel, and the app uses an algorithm to pair users, based on their location, interests, and compatibility. Once you're matched, you can start messaging each other, but no photos can be shared."

"I guess that's kind of nice," Alice said with a shrug. "At least it's keeping people from matching solely on physical appearance."

"I don't know. Seems weird to me." Gigi took a sip of her margarita, thinking about the dating scene and all the app options. She ran a hand over Tux's fluffy black body. He stretched out and yawned. "There are a ton of dating apps that match on compatibility. This one just seems shady. Like it was designed for cheaters."

"Yeah, I could see that." Alice tilted her head, pursing her lips. "So, what happens if you actually want to meet the person you're messaging? How are you supposed to meet if you don't know what that person looks like?"

Paige silently read, swirling her margarita. The ice clinked in her glass like a ticking clock, amping up the suspense. "Okay. So, if both parties agree to meet, the app will again spin a wheel, choosing a specific meeting location and first date for the couple. It also gives them a secret word so they can confirm the person when they meet."

"Really?" Gigi asked. "Like you're just supposed to just walk up to a guy at a restaurant and ask him for a secret password? Or yell out some random word like 'bananas' until your date finds you?

And how are you supposed to know you're not meeting a serial killer?"

Alice gasped at the last question. "Good point!" She stopped knitting for a moment, looking as though she were imagining meeting a murderer for cheeseburgers and fries.

"How are we supposed to know *anyone* we meet isn't a serial killer?" Paige stared at Gigi and Alice like that was an obvious observation. "Most serial killers won't divulge that about themselves."

Gigi scrunched her nose. Paige was right. "Still, the app makes it easy for people to hide their identity. Seems like it would attract people with bad intentions, or just people looking for hookups. Anyone *seriously* looking for love won't use it."

Alice agreed, nodding her head. Paige looked as though she were considering all the reasons someone would be on the app. She set her phone on the coffee table, ate a meatball, and took a slurp of her margarita.

"Yeah, I guess it sounds like more of a hook-up app. But it also sounds like it could be fun. *Spontaneous.*" Paige challenged both Gigi and Alice with a quirk of her brow. "Plus, just because you see a guy's face and know their name before you meet them, doesn't mean they're not a weirdo. My dating history is proof of that. Do you remember the foot-fetish guy?"

Gigi was mid-sip. She covered her mouth, barely stopping herself from spitting her margarita all over Mister Tuxedo. Forcing a swallow, she dabbed her mouth on her sweatshirt sleeve before laughing. "I almost forgot about that guy!"

Alice laughed along. "Oh, that guy was a creepo!"

"Yeah, made me think twice about wearing open-toe shoes on a first date. I had no idea red toenail polish could be a beacon for weirdos." Paige slid back in her chair. She shook her head with a chuckle. "Dating is pretty strange, if you really think about it." She stared at the ceiling, lost in thought. "Like how the heck are we supposed to find true love amongst a mess of strangers? Just because I'm attracted to someone's muscular forearms doesn't mean the guy is going to satisfy all my needs and wants for eternity."

Gigi grinned at Paige's flowery description of dating. She wasn't wrong.

"But that creep gave you great writing inspiration," Alice noted, referring to the villain Paige had created for a romantic suspense novel a few years back—a kidnapper with a penchant for painted toes. The first book in a series that launched her successful writing career.

Paige sat up straight in her chair. "It did, didn't it?"

Gigi immediately shook her head, following Paige's train of thought. "No one needs you to test out this app just to get writing inspiration."

"I bet it would give me some great ideas." Paige's eyes were wide, like she'd just discovered a hundred-dollar bill hidden in her coat pocket.

Gigi tilted her head, knowing she wouldn't change Paige's mind. "Please promise me you'll tell us exactly where you're going if you decide to meet up with someone."

"I'll send you a pin of my location." Paige smirked, and Gigi shook her head. "But let's get back to the topic at hand—your grumpy, rich, hot boss that's currently blowing up your life." Paige leaned against the armrest, setting her chin on her fist. "How do we stop him from being a pain and instead get him to take you on some fancy date that involves a helicopter and a private island?"

Gigi rolled her eyes and laughed. "First of all, that only happens in books."

"Or on *The Bachelor*," Alice chimed in, like that show mirrored real life.

"Another piece of fiction," Gigi replied good-naturedly. All three of them loved *The Bachelor*. When the show was on, their Yappy Hours consisted of watching the latest episodes and dissecting all the drama. "Also, he's my boss. I can't date him. I'd like to stay out of HR and keep my job, thank you very much." Even as she said it, Gigi had to stuff down the memory of being splayed across Harris. She cleared her throat when she remembered the hard planes of his chest and her pulse started snapping.

"Well, that's boring," Paige said, looking disappointed.

"I just need to figure out how to make him back off," Gigi added. "I don't want him making a bunch of changes that are going to mess everything up."

Alice and Paige nodded, their gazes going unfocused, like they'd put on their thinking caps to come up with a way to fix Gigi's conundrum. That's what they did for one another.

Alice tapped her chin. "You're doing the entire Gal's Gift Guide with him?"

"Looks like it," Gigi answered with a nod. "I need a second person to represent the company. Each of the activities is made for groups of two or more. Plus, I need another person to help take pictures and videos for SheTime's social."

"Can you lock him in the office supply closet and bring me instead?" Paige asked, as if this were a good option.

"I'd prefer not to go to jail." Wishing she could do that—but knowing she couldn't—Gigi sipped her drink. "Plus, it needs to be someone from the company and Dean seems intent on sending his brother."

"Why don't you make every single activity completely miserable for Harris until he gives up and sends someone else?" Alice asked as she knitted, her eyes on the needles like she hadn't just come up with an idea that was completely devious . . . and genius.

Gigi and Paige stared at her. Alice was sweet and innocent, but mess with one of her friends and her claws came out.

"That—" Gigi started, lowering her margarita from her lips. "Might work."

Alice smiled mischievously. "What's your event tomorrow? We can brainstorm ideas to make Harris squirm."

Paige jumped up from the chair. "This is going to require another batch of margaritas!" She spun toward the kitchen.

Gigi laughed, the stress of the day melting away. This was why she loved her friends—one of the many reasons. They supported each other through everything, no matter how big or small.

"Tomorrow is Christmas karaoke," Gigi started. "'Merry-oke,' to be exact. And I need an idea for a song. Something completely obnoxious."

Chapter Five

Harris stepped into the dueling piano bar, not excited to spend his Saturday evening surrounded by strangers, especially when he laid eyes on the onslaught of holiday cheer. He'd been to Sing-Alongs Tavern before, many years ago, before he moved to New York. But the usually dimly lit, lively bar had been transformed into a Christmas nightmare, practically glowing from the inside out.

Strands of twinkle lights and green garland covered every surface and most of the ceiling. A large Christmas tree dominated one corner of the bar, adorned with baubles and silver tinsel. Two garishly dressed pianists occupied the dueling pianos, which sat on a raised stage against the back wall. Were they supposed to be elves? Muppets? Harris cringed as the crowd sang along with the pointy-hat-pianists, belting out "Deck the Halls."

"This is going to be a long night," he grumbled to himself, just as a hostess approached, sporting a Santa hat.

"Happy Holidays," she greeted with too much pep, the end of her red hat swinging. "Do you have a reservation? We're completely booked this evening." She gave an apologetic gaze, batting her eyelashes.

"I'm here for SheTime. Should be on the list. Harris Ryan."

"Oh," the hostess perked up again. She scanned her computer screen, clicked, and smiled. "Perfect. I can show you to your table. This way, please."

This was anything but perfect. Still, Harris followed her through the packed bar, weaving through tables occupied with people adorned in tacky Christmas attire. Harris looked to be the only person not dressed in a costume. He smoothed down the front of his collared shirt and adjusted his jacket, wondering when Chicago had lost its sense of style.

"Here you go," the hostess said, setting a menu on the high-top table. "The other rep from SheTime is over by your product display. She can bring you up to speed on the schedule tonight. Your server will be by shortly."

As the hostess wandered off, Harris scanned the bar, past clinking glasses and groups of off-key patrons, singing loudly. The festive madness was already fraying his nerves. Could he get away with a neat whiskey, even though this was a work event? Maybe he'd only stay long enough to see what the company was paying for.

How in the heck would this positively affect their bottom line? He wanted to go straight back to his brownstone and enjoy a stiff glass of aged Kentucky bourbon in peace.

As Harris removed his jacket and hung it on the back of the chair, Gigi appeared. She popped out of the crowd, taking him by surprise.

"You're underdressed!" she yelled her greeting over the singing patrons. Harris turned, immediately losing his train of thought when he took in her outfit. His mouth opened, but there were no words. Gigi outshone the Christmas tree in the corner.

Just like their first encounter, she sported a Christmas sweater, but this one was a holiday billboard—bright red with a huge, fuzzy Christmas tree covering the front. Blinking lights protruded from the tree, glowing in an array of colors. Harris gawked. There had to be a substantial battery pack hidden under her shirt.

"I can't believe I didn't see you coming," he uttered, without thinking.

"What?" She tilted her head, shaking a headband full of sparkling, round ornaments that sat atop her dark, shoulder-length hair like a crown.

"Nothing." He shook his head, thankful when the last chords of "Deck the Halls" ended, and the singing stopped.

As the crowd clapped and found their seats, Gigi dug into the tote bag on her chair. "Didn't Dean send you the details for tonight?" It was a little easier to hear her as the crowd wound down.

"No. He just told me when and where to be."

"Hmm." Gigi smiled, like she had something up her sleeve. "Good thing I brought an extra sweater." She tugged a red-and-green monstrosity from her bag, holding it up for Harris to see. He nearly gagged. The entire front of the sweater was a cartoon-like reindeer head, complete with felt antlers that protruded like sad, crooked fingers.

"Excuse me, what?" he asked, horrified. "What is that for?" She did not expect him to wear that, did she?

"You can throw it on over your shirt. Come on." She shook the sweater, clearly delighted with her reveal. "We don't have much time."

"Time for what? What is happening?"

Tossing the sweater at him, she said, "Before Merry-oke. We're up next."

He caught the shirt, mostly to keep it from falling to the sticky bar floor. "Merry-oke?" he slowly repeated. "Is that what it sounds like?"

"*Exactly* what it sounds like. Christmas karaoke, with the pianos."

He shook his head, taking a step back. "No, no, no, no, no. I didn't sign up for this."

"Actually, you did when you agreed to take Kim's place." Her smile was sweet, but Harris was getting this strange vibe that she was enjoying his discomfort. "Each of the sponsors for tonight's event is competing in Merry-oke and the crowd picks the winner. The winning team gets to donate a thousand dollars to the charity of their choice. SheTime's charity is Toys for Tots, so we need to sing our little hearts out for the kids. Right? You wouldn't want to let down the kids. Would you, Harris?"

"I-I—" he stuttered, gripping the thick sweater in his hand. *I can't do this.* "I don't have a singing voice."

She shook her head, like this was a silly comment. "Everyone has a singing voice. You don't have to be perfect."

"No, really. I don't sing in the shower, in the car, nothing. And I definitely don't sing in public."

"Really? You don't even sing in the shower?"

"Really."

"Well—" She tapped her chin. "That's weird."

Harris scrunched his forehead. "It's not that weird. Not everyone sings." Or likes Christmas. He wasn't a big fan of either.

She shrugged, seeming to accept this. "Well, it's a good thing I love to sing, then. I'm no Mariah Carey, but I can hold a tune. I was in high school choir, and—" Gigi spouted off something about being a soprano and a solo she once got, but the only two words that had jumped out at Harris were . . . *Mariah Carey.*

"What song are we singing?" he asked pointedly, praying to the heavens he was not right about the answer.

Gigi's eyes lit up, matching the blinking lights on her sweater. "The crème de la crème of Christmas songs. The epitome of festive festiveness. The best-selling Christmas song of all time by a female artist. The song that is the official start of every Christmas season."

Harris's pulse quickened with every over-the-top descriptor. "Are we seriously going to sing 'All I Want for Christmas'—"

"Is You!" Gigi clapped her hands in front of her chest, finishing the title of the song with enough vigor to rock Harris back on his heels.

"I don't think so." Harris turned and took a step toward the door. He would not throw on a garishly obnoxious sweater and join Gigi for a Mariah Carey duet. A vision flashed through his head, and he was certain he'd make a complete fool of himself and the company. But before he escaped, Gigi snagged hold of his arm. He was just about to lecture her about the ridiculous road SheTime was on, but she cut him off.

"I already told the coordinator you'd be joining me." There was the slightest bit of panic in her brown eyes, which was the most appropriate response he'd seen yet tonight. Who surprises their new boss with public humiliation?

"You're going to have to retract that statement. You'll be singing a solo tonight." He couldn't get out of the bar fast enough.

"But I—" Gigi's response fell short when the overhead lights dimmed, and a spotlight circled the two of them like a lasso. Harris blinked against the brightness.

"Next to the stage," the announcer began, "will be Gigi Ricci and Harris Ryan, representing the delightful line of premium beauty products from SheTime, which are redefining the notion of self-care. Make sure to check out their holiday gift sets in the sponsored area near the Christmas tree. Pamper someone special in your life with the limited edition sets of body soap and lotions in the fun, festive scents of Christmas Sleigh Ride, Sugar Cookie Dough, and Cozy Cashmere Dreams."

Harris froze, noticing the onslaught of eyes that were now turned on him, wanting him to sing and dance like a circus monkey. He should've run for the door at the first mention of Merry-oke, but now he was linked to SheTime. It wouldn't be a good look if he shook off Gigi's grip, cursed Christmas, and left.

Harris forced a stiff smile for the crowd.

"It won't be that bad," Gigi whispered. "I'll do the singing. Just put on the sweater and you can handle the sleigh bells. You can chime in and sing if you feel comfortable."

"Comfortable?" he repeated the word like he was being thrown to the wolves.

"Come on. You got this." Gigi slid her hand down his arm and laced her fingers in his. Her touch sent a jolt of electricity straight through him, pushing him into a new realm of panic, but she didn't let him focus on whatever he was feeling for long. In the next instant, Gigi tightened her grip and turned toward the pianos, taking him with her.

Harris stumbled forward, not believing his current predicament. The only thing that kept him moving—outside of Gigi's steel grip—was what Dean had said about Gigi. His brother thought highly of her. And in this moment, all Harris could do was trust his brother's opinion of the woman dragging him to his worst nightmare.

Hoots, hollers, and clapping filled the bar as Gigi and Harris made their way on stage. Harris wanted to disappear, but Gigi waved at the crowd like this was a normal Saturday night. She only let go of Harris's hand when they stood in front of the two pianos. Before them were two mic stands and a computer screen with lyrics. Harris scanned the crowd. They were analyzing him as though they might've found a hair in their dinner.

"You all are in for a treat with this one," the announcer said from the DJ booth in the corner. "Are you all ready for a little Mariah Carey?" A ripple of excitement rolled through the bar. Gigi waved again at the crowd, this time with both hands. Harris wondered if she'd pull out pom-poms and a cheerleader routine before the music even started.

Gigi stepped close to him, looking at ease and eager—completely opposite from what he felt. "Put on your sweater." She smiled, pointing to the monstrosity Harris forgot he was holding. "I'll get the sleigh bells."

She left him, walking to the back of the stage. Horrified, Harris slid the sweater on, mostly to hide his face for a few seconds. Could he stay hidden? Tucked inside the cartoon reindeer while Gigi put on a show? Knowing that would *guarantee* he ended up on some stupid, viral Instagram reel, he yanked the scratchy sweater in place and finished fixing his collar just as Gigi returned.

"Here." She handed him a leather strap with silver bells. "Shake the bells in rhythm with the beat after the first chorus ends." When he didn't reply, she tipped her head and added, "You know the song, right?"

"Yeah, I know it," he said begrudgingly. It was the national anthem of Christmas. Everyone knew it. It was played to death between Thanksgiving and Christmas every year.

"Great." Her bright reply confirmed nothing would keep her from enjoying this. Nodding at the announcer, Gigi grabbed a mic out of a stand.

Harris's heart bounded as the announcer added a few more details, noting that the crowd could vote for their favorite team using a text code on their phone. He also said this was livestreaming on Facebook, and Harris immediately wished for a trap door that would open up and drop him into the basement. Did this club even have a basement? For a second, he closed his eyes, blocking out the beaming spotlight, wanting the next few minutes to be a distant memory.

When one pianist started with the first telltale notes of the song, Harris opened his eyes, taking in the crowd. They were chatting and drinking, only half paying attention. But when Gigi sang the first few notes, the crowd quieted, turning to watch. Harris did too.

Her voice wasn't good; it was stunning. The clear, melodic tones cut through the room, demanding attention. Harris, who'd been ready to cringe through the entire ordeal, found himself instantly captivated. He hadn't expected this from someone who'd just moments ago had said she "was no Mariah Carey" and then dragged him on stage against his will.

In her twinkling Christmas sweater and black leggings, Gigi effortlessly worked the crowd. She strode across the stage, singing into the microphone like a pro. With each note, her eyes sparkled with joy, which spread, catching everyone in its wake. The audience quickly joined in, clapping in rhythm. When they sang along, Gigi glanced at Harris, urging him with a smile, and he remembered the strap of bells in his hand.

Still in awe, he started shaking the bells, almost mindlessly, thinking this woman had the voice of an angel. But more than that, her courage and charisma had enchanted the entire bar, as if magic dripped from her tongue. There was no way Harris could do anything of the sort. He could take control in the boardroom, but outside of that, he'd never volunteer to be in the spotlight. Yet, somehow here he was, sharing it with Gigi, his panic lessening as her joy and voice infused the room.

He kept up his part, shaking the bells through the rest of the tune, and as the end of the song neared, Gigi belted out the last lines, her voice reaching a triumphant crescendo. Harris bent back in amazement, and the crowd roared in response. A sea of delighted faces leapt to their feet.

Gigi took a humble bow. Then she turned toward Harris, still glowing from her performance. Their eyes met to share a moment of triumph and surprise.

As the applause faded, Gigi walked over to Harris. "Great job!" she exclaimed. "We killed it!"

Harris, still processing the rollercoaster of emotions that had shot through him in the past ten minutes, managed a smile. "*You* killed it."

"Couldn't do it without the bells." She grinned, giving Harris this strange sense of accomplishment. A warmth spread through his chest. He nodded, caught in the moment. Why was he drawn to this woman? He'd felt it the first time he met her, too, in the elevator. She was gorgeous, of course. Bright, inquisitive chocolate-brown eyes. Soft curves and legs that went on for days. But it was more than that. She had this bubble of magnetic energy that grabbed everyone around her, including him.

Harris shook his head, dislodging his thoughts. His logical mind grabbed hold of his emotions, reminding him of professional boundaries.

You're her boss.

He was only in Chicago temporarily, specifically to help his brother. There was no need to consider his attraction to Gigi or what that might mean.

With a crackle of the speakers, the announcer declared Harris and Gigi the new Merry-oke leaders.

Gigi laughed and clapped her hands together. Her eyes shone, catching Harris in their wake. "Looks like we have a shot at winning this thing."

Harris nodded. As the crowd closed in, offering congratulations and clinks of their glasses, he slipped away, going back to the table where he peeled off the sweater, along with the glimmer of attraction stirring in his gut. He was here to help his brother. Nothing else. He kept telling himself that, even as the echoes of Gigi's voice and bright smile replayed through his mind.

Chapter Six

Gigi stared at Harris across the boardroom table, wishing she had lasers in her eyes. Tightening her grip on her pen, she imagined burning Harris with her thoughts, searing zigzags in his expensive suit and possibly torching the ends of his perfectly mussed hair.

Instead, she sighed, composing herself so the words she really wanted to say didn't leave her mouth. She glanced around the long table occupied by the other members of the SheTime team. Then she focused on Harris. "So, you think the best decision is to cut costs wherever possible?"

"Not wherever possible." Harris leaned on the table, linking his hands together. "Just where it makes sense. And I think it makes sense to cut cost out of the packaging and ingredients. Also, to reassess our spend on marketing and events."

"Interesting." Gigi eased back in her chair, steepling her hands. She tapped her fingertips together in silence, long enough to feel the energy in the room shift. One of the sales reps coughed, and then awkwardly apologized for doing so. Jeremiah, from finance, looked back and forth between Harris and Gigi as though a fire had started and someone better put it out. The others munched on snacks, tentatively chewing as they waited to see where this was going.

The team had been in the boardroom all morning, analyzing products and marketing, reviewing spend and results. Gigi was on the verge of losing her mind, but Harris seemed unfazed. Every time she challenged him, he came back with a confident and solid answer. *Even though he was wrong.*

"You think we'll grow sales and market share by reducing the quality of the product we make?" She stilled her fingers.

"You think we should manufacture products that don't meet internal profit requirements? Or support marketing that doesn't grow our bottom line?" he countered.

She narrowed her eyes, not appreciating how he'd answered her question with more questions. "There's a difference between cutting corners and finding smarter, more sustainable solutions. We can't compromise the quality of our products. That's what sets SheTime apart in the beauty space."

"We're not compromising quality. We're optimizing. Besides, consumers want value."

She shook her head. "Value, yes. But not at the expense of quality. Our consumers *want* eco-friendly, cruelty-free, top-quality products that give them a luxurious experience. And I have the research that says so."

"Look, Gigi, I commend your passion, but we need to be realistic. The market is tough, and we need to make strategic decisions."

"All the more reason not to compromise," she replied. They locked gazes, a silent battle of wills fighting across the table until Jeremiah cleared his throat.

"Are we going to break for lunch?" Jeremiah asked, like he was starving.

Gigi leaned forward, ignoring Jeremiah. "You know what else gives us an edge, Harris?" He raised a brow, urging her on. "SheTime isn't about selling quantity. We provide quality. We build community. Consumers want a brand they can connect with, not just something off a drugstore shelf. We make premium beauty products, and our marketing and events build a community around our brand."

Harris sighed and sat back in his chair, seemingly unimpressed. "Gigi, I've seen the success of the events, but they're resource intensive, and I'm not convinced they're the most efficient way to allocate our budget. We need to explore other, more cost effective, and measurable avenues."

Gigi quietly huffed. What did this man not understand about their products and market? They'd officially talked in circles, landing right back where they started this morning. After Merry-oke, Gigi thought she'd convinced Harris to back off. He'd obviously been uncomfortable at the event and onstage, like he'd desperately wanted to be anywhere else. Then, he'd emailed her afterward, letting her know that Dean and his daughter would fill in for him at the event on Sunday. She thought she'd won after belting out Mariah Carey in a Christmas sweater, but this morning, Harris entered the boardroom like he'd spent the past twenty-four hours figuring out how he could change the business.

But Gigi was determined to stand her ground. She'd run circles forever if she had to.

Gigi sat up, making her chair roll closer to the table. "The Gal's Gift Guide is measurable. We sold out of all the holiday gift sets featured at Merry-oke. Plus, the video of us singing went viral, with SheTime's logo and banner in the background. We sold out of product and got over a million impressions in one day. That sounds measurable to me."

Harris looked slightly sickened. It wasn't the reaction she'd been going for, but at least it was some kind of reaction other than stubbornness and mansplaining.

"So, about lunch?" Jeremiah interrupted their stare-off, glancing at his watch. "If I don't eat soon, I'm going to gnaw on a pencil."

"We should break for lunch," Harris agreed, tapping a hand on the table. "Actually, let's take the afternoon to process our discussions and we'll reconvene in the morning. I'd like everyone to come back with one idea within your own job function that will increase margins."

Margins, margins, margins. That's all Harris seemed to care about.

Gigi closed her notebook, grabbed her pen, and shoved both into her briefcase, frustrated that she'd spent an entire morning justifying everything she'd worked tirelessly to implement. She was going to need a sweet treat to counterbalance all the bullpucky she'd just consumed. Maybe Paige and Alice could meet for an emergency lunch at their favorite ice cream shop?

Harris interrupted her daydreams of white chocolate ice cream covered in gummy bears. "Gigi, can you send me all the details for tonight's event? Including attire." He looked a little salty about the last part, and Gigi internally smirked, remembering his disdain for the reindeer sweater.

"Of course," she replied, wishing Dean would just take Harris's place for the rest of the events. Dean was happy-go-lucky. He was fun and supportive. He was everything Harris was not.

Over lunch, she vented to her friends about the morning's developments.

"Keep at it," Paige encouraged through a mouthful of blue moon ice cream. "Keep showing him you mean business. He'll back off, eventually. You're the bomb. Just keep proving that."

"You are totally the bomb," Alice agreed, licking her lips before digging her spoon back into her frozen yogurt. "What's tonight's event? We need to brainstorm more ideas to make him wish he'd stayed home."

By the time Gigi returned to her desk, she had committed to her plan: make Harris squirm while excelling at her job. And since he disliked dressing up, she doubled down on that aspect.

Clicking her mouse, she opened an email and addressed it to Harris.

To: harrison.ryan@ryan&ryan.com

From: gianna.ricci@ryan&ryan.com

Re: Monday event details–Gals' Gift Guide

Good afternoon, Harris,

Please see below for details concerning tonight's Gals' Gift Guide event. The main sponsor of tonight's event is Christmas Village, Inc. We'll be competing in a gingerbread house-making competition, using the Christmas Village baking kits. I thought we could create a gingerbread spa. Please dress casually. I will bring matching company attire for us to wear. We have logoed pink silk robes, fluffy slippers, and sleep masks that will be perfect for this event.

Please meet me at the Four Seasons on Delaware Place at 6:00 p.m. sharp.

Sincerely,

Gigi

Gigi chuckled quietly as she wrapped up the email, but before she sent it, she played around with her signature. She erased "Sincerely," and replaced it with:

If you have any questions, please ask someone else,
Gigi

This made her laugh out loud. Sometimes, when she was frustrated, she would type up an email expressing what she *really* wanted to say. She never sent it. It just made her feel better to get a little snark off her chest. But before she could correct her signature, Jeremiah walked up behind her.

"Have you seen the new Netflix documentary where the kidnapper lures his victims into his van with the promise of free margaritas, chips, and guac?"

Gigi moved her mouse, intending to minimize her email so Jeremiah didn't read her snarky signature over her shoulder. He was the biggest office gossip. Though Jeremiah had great taste in murder mysteries, and that sounded like something Gigi needed to watch.

"I haven't, but I—" She clicked her mouse and the whoosh sound that followed knocked her stomach to the floor. "I did *not* just do that." But she had. She'd accidentally emailed Harris before correcting her signature. "No, no, no, no, no!"

"Well, you should watch it," Jeremiah continued, unaware of the colossal mistake Gigi had just made. "It's amazing what people will do for a free margarita and guac. Plus, the twist at the end will throw you for a loop. I didn't see it coming at all."

Panic rising, Gigi stood, pushing her chair out from under her. "Hold that thought." She left Jeremiah and ran for the elevator, not sure what she should do. Harris didn't seem to have a funny bone in his body. He would not read her email and then chuckle at her signature like she'd made a hilarious knock-knock joke. This morning confirmed they didn't see eye to eye, and Gigi was getting the feeling he was searching for reasons to call her out. This would definitely give him a reason.

It was one thing to make Harris uncomfortable while still elevating sales and social reach. But blatantly disrespecting her new boss in writing? That wouldn't go over well. As she impatiently waited for the elevator to reach the tenth floor, Gigi pictured Harris scowling at his computer before forwarding the email straight to HR.

How was she going to explain this?

Getting off the elevator and nearing his office, Gigi wondered if she could blame her signature on dictation. At least, that was somewhat believable. She could say she was dictating the email and her computer picked up on a conversation in the next cubicle. She didn't realize the mistake until she hit send. Then she could laugh about it, even if Harris didn't crack a smile.

You need to be extra careful when speaking your truth in an email, she scolded herself.

Harris's door was halfway open. She knocked and stepped in. "Harris? Can I talk to you for a second?"

He was at his desk, though he wasn't looking at his computer. Instead, his chair was rotated and tipped back. He had one leg crossed over the other and was staring blankly out the floor-to-ceiling windows into the abyss of Chicago. He slowly turned his head toward her, but didn't offer a greeting.

Had he read her email? Was he stewing over ways to reprimand her?

"I just wanted to explain the email I just sent," she said, nerves prickling her insides. "I didn't mean the signature I put at the bottom. I—"

He put one finger to his mouth and shushed her.

Gigi stood there, bewildered. She blinked at him, her mouth going slightly agape, trying to process what had just happened. Was this some new power move? Had he seriously just shushed her?

Harris slowly rotated toward her, his expression shifting from stern to conspiratorial. Without saying a word, he crooked a finger, gesturing for Gigi to come close. Suspiciously, she approached his desk. As she neared, Harris's stern exterior softened.

"I was just going to call you," he spoke softly. "I was hoping you could help me with something." Tugging on the lapel of his sport coat, he eased it away from his chest. Gigi's confusion deepened. What was he doing? Was he going to yank a pink slip out of a hidden pocket?

But Gigi stilled when she saw what was hidden under his jacket. She tilted her head to get a better look and make sure her eyes weren't deceiving her. Curled up on Harris's chest was a tiny, fluffy, orange . . . sleeping kitten.

Gigi sucked in a breath. "You have a kitten?" Her eyes widened in surprise.

Harris kept his gaze on the fluffball. "He's not mine. I found him on the way to lunch. He was in a bush next to the Thai place, screaming his lungs out. I wasn't sure what to do with him, but I couldn't leave him out there in the cold, so I brought him back to the office. Just cleaned him up and got him to eat a little something. I wasn't sure what to get, but grabbed a can of tuna at the corner market."

"Oh, my goodness," she whispered, shocked. Gigi had nearly tripped over her own feet getting to Harris's office, and this was the last thing she expected to find.

Harris nodded toward the edge of his desk. A dirty hand towel was folded up next to a small paper plate with a lump of canned tuna. "I put him in my jacket to warm him up and he fell asleep. I was trying not to wake him. Wanted to let him sleep."

Harris's gaze connected with hers, evaporating Gigi's panic and all thoughts of the email.

"You shushed me for a kitten," she said, confirming the fact for herself.

"I figured the poor thing needs some rest." He quirked a smile and Gigi's disdain for Harris melted—a little. He was harboring a stray kitten in his jacket. How could her heart not soften for him?

At least this showed a bit of humanity. He wasn't one hundred percent a grump. Maybe just ninety-eight percent? She straightened her face, not wanting Harris to catch her train of thought.

"You said you really like cats. I was hoping you could help me get supplies for him?" Harris asked, throwing Gigi for another loop.

"Supplies?"

"Yeah, I'm going to call some local rescues, but I was thinking he could stay with me until he gets a permanent home. I don't want him to have to stay in a shelter. I'll need supplies for home and for the office. I don't want to leave him at home all day by himself."

Gigi's knees went weak at his admission. She wobbled on her heels. One ankle gave way, and she shuffled forward, steading herself with a hand on the edge of Harris's desk.

"You okay?" Alarm captured Harris's features.

"Yeah, yeah. Totally." She stood up straight, bracing her traitorous legs. "That's . . . that's really nice of you."

He shrugged a shoulder, brushing off her compliment. "I just want him to be safe and find a good home."

She smiled at Harris, and he returned it. It was probably the first genuine smile she'd shared with him since their introduction in the elevator.

"You wouldn't be interested in another cat, would you?" he asked.

Gigi's heart squeezed. "I wish I could take him." She stood up straight, tugging at the edge of her sweater, which was purple with green polka dots. No embroidered cats today. "My apartment building doesn't allow pets."

"Oh," Harris replied. "I just assumed you had a cat or two."

She grinned. "I'll gladly be a crazy cat lady someday."

Harris raised his brow, like he should stuff a foot in his mouth. "I didn't mean that offensively."

"I didn't take offense. I can't wait until I can have cats. But right now, I don't spend enough time at home. It wouldn't be fair to any animal. But I spoil my friend Alice's cat, Tux."

The sharp angles of Harris's expression eased. "That's nice." He looked at her with something that resembled adoration. It wasn't the typical response she received when she told men about her love of cats. "I was never allowed any pets growing up."

"Ever?"

Harris shook his head. "My dad liked the house to stay spotless. Having a pet was never an option."

Gigi's curiosity piqued at this break in Harris's all-business demeanor. She wanted to know more, and started to ask him if he had any pets now, but the little orange fluff woke. The kitten raised his head and let out a pitiful meow.

"Oh, my." Gigi pressed her hand to her chest, her heart expanding for the little stray. "Can I hold him?"

"Sure." Harris carefully gathered the little guy. "How do you know it's a 'him'?"

"Over eighty percent of orange cats are male." Gigi swept around the side of his desk, beyond excited for the little ball of sunshine that was brightening her day.

"Interesting," Harris said, offering up the kitten.

"Look at your little face," she said between tight lips, bending toward the adorable furball, not able to contain her excitement. The kitten squeaked again.

Harris chuckled and gently handed the bundle of fur to Gigi. She held the kitten up before her, staring into his sweet, pleading blue eyes. "You're okay now. We're going to find you a wonderful home. No more cold nights on the street. Your life will be filled with so many treats, plush cat beds set in warm sunshine, and endless snuggles." The kitten meowed at her, a little less pathetic this time, and she pulled him to her chest. He clung to her sweater, clawing up to nestle next to her neck. She pressed him close, and he purred. Gigi gasped at the sweetness of it all, catching Harris's gaze to share the moment.

"He likes you," he said, with a tenderness that gave her pause.

Gigi scratched behind the kitten's ears, and the purring increased. "I like him too."

Harris smiled at her. Something lighter replaced the tension that had lingered between them in the boardroom. Gigi felt a shift, a truce of sorts. Maybe they weren't destined to be at each other's throats all the time?

"I should probably get him some supplies." Harris broke the momentary silence.

"Right," Gigi agreed, her mind still catching up with the unexpected turn of events.

"Can you help me with that? I'm not sure what he all needs."

"Sure. I know a great pet store nearby. I could run over there now, if you'd like."

"You don't have to go shopping for me. I don't want you to feel like you're my assistant."

"It's not a problem," she replied, appreciating his awareness with the ask. "I'd be happy to help. Actually, the shopping part sounds fun. And I know the pet store delivers. I can have the supplies sent to your house and here to the office."

"That'd be great," Harris replied. "I'd really appreciate that."

They exchanged a look, a shared understanding that extended beyond the immediate task. Maybe, just maybe, there was more to discover beneath the surface of Harris's prickly presence.

"It's not a problem," Gigi said, giving the kitten a kiss on his head before handing him back to Harris. "Plus, it'll be great to have an office kitten until we can find him a home. Maybe someone in the office will adopt him?"

She smiled at the thought, and Harris nodded. But as she turned to leave his office, Gigi stopped, remembering what she'd come here for. She swallowed, the truth bubbling inside her, ready to spill out. "I sent you an email with a sarcastic signature. I'm sorry about that. I don't want to be disrespectful. Sometimes I type snarky signatures on emails just to make myself laugh, but I always delete them and write something professional. I just wanted you to know that before you read it. Please ignore my ill-placed sarcasm."

Harris looked perplexed for a moment. Then he nodded, rolling his big hand over the tiny kitten's head. The kitten closed his eyes in appreciation. "Consider it ignored."

Chapter Seven

The kitten's supplies arrived at Harris's doorstep not long after he got home, which Harris greatly appreciated. He'd given Gigi his credit card and told her to buy whatever she saw fit. The supplies could go with the kitten to his new home or be donated to a shelter, and Gigi had done a great job. She'd gotten all the necessities without going overboard. When Gigi had returned Harris's credit card, she'd given him a breakdown of all the supplies, as well as tips to get the kitten comfortable at home. She was very knowledgeable and thoughtful. Now, Harris had the wire kennel setup in his bedroom, complete with a fuzzy bed, toys, food and water dishes, and a litter box.

"Put him in the kennel when you aren't home," Gigi had said. "It will make him feel safe. Plus, I have a feeling he's going to be worn out from today. He'll probably sleep the whole time you're at the gift guide event. And leave a light on for him so he can check out his surroundings."

Harris clicked on the lamp next to his bed before bending down toward the kennel. "I'll only be gone for a few hours, okay?" The kitten blinked up at him from the fluffy cat bed he'd curled into. He was trying hard to keep his eyes open, and Harris smiled, knowing his little belly was full of organic, grain-free paté. He was safe, warm, and sleepy. "I'll be back tonight. I just have a work event to go to." Harris paused, laughing at himself. He was telling this kitten about his schedule. But it was kind of nice to have someone to report to.

After shoveling some takeout leftovers into his mouth, Harris threw on his jacket and hit the streets, toward the Four Seasons. The hotel wasn't far from his brownstone. Maybe a fifteen-minute walk. He'd be right on time, according to the information Gigi had put in her email. As he walked the frosty sidewalks, Harris smirked, thinking of the signature she'd apologized for.

If you have any questions, ask someone else.

If he'd read that without her explanation, Harris would've likely gotten annoyed and written her up. Instead, he'd chuckled. How many times had he wanted to respond to an email with his honest thoughts? Put someone in their place without the use of corporate jargon? It happened daily. Actually, Gigi's idea to type what she really wanted to say—just to get it off her chest—was genius, as long as the email was corrected before being sent. Harris might have to try that himself. It could lift stress from his day. Not to mention, it would be very entertaining.

Navigating the hotel lobby, Harris followed signs to the ballroom, though he knew where he was going. The reception for his dad's third marriage had been at the Four Seasons. He specifically remembered his dad's new wife going on and on about how the peach roses in her extravagant centerpieces clashed with the silver tablecloths. Harris didn't know what she was talking about. Did peach clash with silver? But she'd complained enough that the hotel staff had switched out all the table clothes to a mute gold a half hour before the reception.

Harris hadn't been back to the hotel since and wasn't necessarily in the mood for a stuffy event tonight. So, when he stepped into the ballroom, he huffed a laugh.

The high ceiling with intricate molding was the same, framed by tall windows and rich burgundy drapes. But Christmas chaos muted the formality of the room. It had possibly been the first time in years that Christmas had made Harris smile.

Life-size, colorful wooden cutouts of Santa, snowmen, reindeer, and trees lined the edges of the ballroom. Long tables filled the center, each covered in red plastic and topped with bowls of candy. Spiced ginger filled the air, and the crowd in the hallway was filtering in, picking up packets at the entrance and claiming seats. Harris spotted Gigi and walked toward her. She was putting the finishing touches on the SheTime product display in the sponsored area. Even though her back was turned to him, she couldn't be missed.

Over dark jeans, Gigi sported a baby-pink silk robe and matching fuzzy slippers. When she turned toward him, Harris eyed the sleep mask, which was pulled up on her forehead. It had the SheTime logo and the words *Hello, Gorgeous* embroidered on it.

Harris stopped before her, considering how passionate she was about her job. Gigi seemed more invested in the business than he'd ever been, even though his last name made up the entirety of Ryan & Ryan.

"Just finishing up here," Gigi said, setting down a stack of brochures.

"It looks great," Harris replied. The holiday gift sets were displayed amongst white-flocked Christmas trees decorated with shiny pink ornaments. Fake snow covered the table.

Gigi squinted her eyes, shooting him a tentative look. "Was that a compliment?"

"It was."

She shrugged before grinning. "I'll take it." Turning toward the ballroom entrance, Gigi pointed toward the miniature store setup, which contained an array of products supplied by the event sponsors. There was already a line to the cashier. "We delivered a pallet of product this time, but if we run out, I put a QR code on these brochures so customers can just scan them with their phones. It'll take them directly to our website to purchase."

"Sounds like you've got it all handled."

She sighed. "I hope so."

"And we're going to be building a gingerbread house?"

"Yep. At the table closest to the store, with the rest of the sponsors." She glanced at her watch. "We start in ten minutes. We'll have a half hour to build our gingerbread spa and then all the houses created by the sponsors will be displayed for the rest of the night. The public can vote for their favorite."

He slid a hand into his coat pocket. "The favorite gets to donate to a charity, again?"

"Look at you." She put fists on her hips, scrunching her robe and drawing Harris's attention to her hourglass shape. "You catch on fast."

He broke his stare, chasing away indecent thoughts, and looked toward the sponsored table, which was filling up. "We should get over there. You said you brought me a robe?"

"I did." Gigi dipped down and retrieved a tote bag from underneath the table. "I picked out a navy one for you. Figured it would complement your serious business-man vibes." She pulled a robe from the bag, a sarcastic glint in her eyes.

Harris removed his winter jacket. "That's much better than a reindeer sweater," he replied, accepting the robe. Gigi took his jacket, folded it up, and tucked it under the table.

"I've got slippers too." As she half disappeared under the tablecloth, searching for the rest of his outfit, Harris slid the robe over his gray Henley. It was tight over his arms and across his shoulders, but he adjusted and tugged it into place, hoping it wouldn't rip.

Gigi crawled out from under the table, setting a pair of plush navy slippers before him. When she looked up, she froze, still crouched on the carpet.

"What?" he asked. "Did I rip a seam?"

Gigi chuckled and stood. "I grabbed the biggest size we had, but the robe looks more like a blazer on you."

He looked down at the silky hem hitting just below his hip. "Perfect fit," he deadpanned. Gigi laughed with genuine amusement, and for a moment, their gazes locked. Something had shifted between them this afternoon. Maybe the kitten had lessened the friction? Harris could still picture the way Gigi had swooped in, immediately going soft at the sight of the stray animal and wanting to do everything she could to help him.

He smiled. The usual tightness in his chest eased.

"It's a little snug," he admitted.

Gigi stepped close and tugged at the lapel with both hands. As she did, her fingers rolled over his chest. "These robes weren't meant for big, strong men."

He swallowed, noting how her fingers had lingered for a second longer than necessary. Furthermore, he noted how he'd enjoyed that extra second.

"Tomorrow, I'll order you a men's XL tall, just in case we use these robes for other events." Gigi gave him a friendly pat on the chest before stepping back.

"I'll manage." He cleared his throat. "As long as the slippers don't cut off circulation to my toes."

"You should be good there. I grabbed a size bigger than what Dean wears."

Harris removed his boots and slid into the slippers. The cozy fleece surrounded his socked feet, and he gave Gigi a thumbs-up. "They fit."

"Good. Nothing worse than uncomfortable shoes." She handed him a sleep mask embroidered with the words *Sleeping Beauty*. He grinned and anchored it on his forehead, just like Gigi's mask.

Dressed for bedtime, they walked toward the sponsored table and prepped their area. As they did, Gigi explained her grand vision for a gingerbread spa, complete with candy cane lounge chairs and licorice pool noodles. Her animated descriptions entertained Harris, and to his surprise, he even made a few suggestions of his own. Her excitement peaked when he suggested adding a gumdrop hot tub. When the timed event started, they moved into an easy rhythm, since they'd already agreed on their individual tasks, and as they constructed their creation, light conversation flowed.

"You got everything you need for the kitten?" Gigi asked, piping royal icing onto the outer edge of one gingerbread wall. "The pet shop said to call if you need anything else."

Harris nodded. "He's all set. Settled in quickly at the house and was asleep when I left. Thanks for rounding up all his supplies."

"No problem. It was fun to do some kitty shopping." Gigi's chocolate eyes glimmered. She popped a peppermint in her mouth and rolled it around. "I can't wait to see him tomorrow at the office. Have you named him yet?"

Harris looked up from where he'd been intently adjusting the candy cane armrest of a lounge chair. "I wasn't going to name him."

"What? Why not?"

"I don't want—" Harris paused. A flicker of vulnerability pulsed through him. He brushed it off. "I don't want him to get confused when he goes to his new home, and they re-name him." It was one thing to house the kitten and keep him safe. It was another to give him a name. Harris wouldn't get attached. Getting attached to anything or anyone was bound to end in heartache. He'd lost enough people in his life to know.

"We can't just call him kitten." Gigi furrowed her brow, looking appalled by Harris's suggestion.

He grabbed a handful of gumdrops from one of the candy bowls and assessed the color options in the palm of his hand, delaying his response. When he finally picked a purple candy, he replied with, "How about you name him?"

Gigi's eyes widened. She stopped piping. "Really?"

"Yes. You name him. Otherwise, I'm going to keep calling him 'kitten.' Besides, you're the one with the marketing background. You'll be much more creative than me."

Gigi's mouth gaped. A little dollop of icing dropped from her pipette. "I'd love to!" She went back to drawing frosting shingles on the roof, energized by her new task. A bright smile captured her face, pushing warmth through Harris's chest, and for the next ten minutes, Gigi led the conversation, rattling off name ideas. *Garfield. Tank. Rufus. Archie. Cookie. Lovebug.* Harris didn't shoot down a single name. He just listened and nodded as Gigi justified and then dismissed each option.

"Oh! I've got it!" She gasped, setting down the frosting bag. Harris situated the last gumdrop on the edge of the hot tub. "Rudolph!"

He squinted at that one. "Rudolph?"

"Yes, it's perfect!" She ripped off a piece of licorice and threw it in her mouth. "You found him just before Christmas. He's a bit of a misfit since he was a stray. Plus, I know he's going to blossom into the most special kitten. He'd be a perfect Rudolph."

"Hmm," he hummed, his initial reaction wavering. He liked the meaning behind the name.

"Plus, we can call him Rudy."

Plastic crinkled as Harris unwrapped a peppermint. He enjoyed Gigi's awaiting stare as he did. "I like it," he conceded.

"Rudy, it is." Gigi shrugged her shoulders in delight. "Rudy, the cutie."

He chuckled and Gigi bent forward, angling the frosting bag at the front of the gingerbread masterpiece. She started making the sign, determination clear in her features as she spelled out The Sweet Spa. Harris watched, admiring the effort she was putting into the task at hand. He was also somewhat stunned that this woman had gotten him to enjoy a Christmas activity *and* to like the name she'd given his temporary kitten. He couldn't remember the last time he'd actually enjoyed a little holiday cheer.

Harris leaned back in his chair, watching her create. "You're really good at this." He tapped the sticky peppermint between his thumb and forefinger.

Gigi glanced over, a pleased smile on her face. "It's all about the details, right?"

"Right." He couldn't agree more. Which caught him off guard because he'd spent the last few days criticizing all the details Gigi was getting wrong with SheTime. Was he overlooking what she brought to the company? "Dean said you started at Ryan & Ryan as a product manager for the men's bar soap line?" he prompted, wanting to learn more about her.

She kept her eyes on her task. "I did. That was a little over seven years ago. It was my foot in the door, and I was grateful for the opportunity, because I really wanted to work at Ryan & Ryan. I'd been working as a marketing associate for a small company, but there wasn't much room to grow there. But once I started at Ryan & Ryan, I knew pretty quickly it wasn't the position I wanted forever. There's only so much room for creativity in that space. It's mostly centered on making a good product for the lowest cost." She gave him a quick glance, seeming to acknowledge the extensive conversations they'd had that morning about expense reductions. "While I was managing the bar soap line, I started writing down all the ideas I was getting for women's beauty products. Stuff I'd buy as a consumer. Those notes morphed into a business plan, and one night, a couple of glasses of wine gave me a boost of courage. I sent the business plan to your brother. He liked it and offered me a product manager position once the new division was formed. The next year, I started as the marketing director."

Harris raised a brow and caught her eye. "You created the business plan for SheTime?" Dean hadn't mentioned that seemingly important piece to Harris.

"I actually enjoy data when I can put it to good use." She gave a crooked grin. "My market analysis helped me find a niche in the industry and an area the company could thrive in." She swooped the cursive frosting at the end of the spa sign and eased back to access her work, poking her tongue out as she did. Harris was so focused on Gigi that he jerked when she twisted toward him.

"You were definitely keeping a secret from me," she said, her stare turning serious.

"I—" Harris's heart bounded, caught off guard. Had Dean told Gigi that Harris had suggested dissolving SheTime and moving the team to other positions within Ryan & Ryan? Was she concerned about getting thrown back into a world of boring bar soap? Or losing her job?

"You've been hiding your secret talent for gingerbread architecture." She smirked. "I mean, look at the masterpiece we created." She waved her hand at the structure proudly.

Harris smiled, covering the anxiety that had hit him. Could he look Gigi in the eye with a clear conscience once he convinced his father and brother that dissolving SheTime was best for the company? "No hidden talent here. I was just following your lead." He tipped forward and added the peppermint to the middle of the wreath on the door.

"I disagree." Gigi shot him a wink and a sidelong glance. "You're definitely keeping secrets."

Harris forced his smile to stay in place as guilt stirred in his gut. He tossed a gumdrop in his mouth, chewing the candy like the sticky truth. This was exactly why he maintained a strict boundary between personal and professional matters. Now he was second-guessing business decisions he'd made with cold, hard facts.

He swallowed the gumdrop. Gigi was a complication he couldn't afford. So why couldn't he resist being pulled into her orbit?

Chapter Eight

Gigi stared at her phone. She opened the group text with her friends, not sure how to explain her evening with Harris. Yesterday, she was determined to sabotage his involvement in the Gals' Gift Guide. But then he'd saved a kitten. And she'd had fun building a gingerbread house with him. What parallel universe was she living in? And how did she get here?

Gigi: Hey, ladies! Survived last night's gift guide event.

Paige: Spill the tea, G! Did the robe and fuzzy slippers put him over the edge? Send him running into the abyss?

Alice: Details! Did Mr. Grumpy Pants actually build a gingerbread house with you? Was he scowling the whole time?

Gigi: The robe and slippers didn't scare him. We made a gingerbread spa. With a gumdrop hot tub and candy cane lounge chairs.

Paige: Excuse me, what?!

Gigi: I know, right? He was actually . . . pleasant?

Alice: Did you make Mr. Grinch's heart grow three sizes?!

Paige: Wow . . . we really need to up our game with our sabotage tactics.

Gigi: LOL. Also, he let me name his kitten.

Paige: What in the heck happened last night?! Do we need an emergency Yappy Hour?!

Alice: OMG! He's going to pick you up in his helicopter and take you to dinner on a private island. I just know it!

Gigi: That's not happening. But we might need an emergency Yappy Hour. I need a plan for tomorrow's event. Wine and apps at The Glass Cork? 5:30?

Paige: I'll be there! What's tomorrow's event? I want to brainstorm.

Alice: I might be a little late! Got to finish inventory at the bookstore, but will be there as soon as I can. Order me that Pinot Gris we got last time. Yum yum!

Gigi: Yay! See you guys later! BTW, tomorrow's event is a horse-drawn carriage ride.

Paige: You're going on a horse-drawn carriage ride with Mr. Grumpy Sea-glass Eyes?! We DEFINITELY need an emergency Yappy Hour!

Alice: Ohhhhhhh, that's better than a helicopter ride!

Gigi: You two are crazy and I love every second of it!

Paige: See you at 5:30! Alice, you better not be late, cause I can only stay for an hour—got a hot date with a match from GambleOnLove. Well, I guess I won't know if he's hot or not until I meet him.

Gigi: PAIGE! No!

Alice: What if it's the senator??

Gigi: At least tell us his username . . .

Paige: hoosier_daddy

Gigi: OMG, you are definitely getting kid-napped.

"You are the handsomest boy I've ever seen," Gigi cooed to the big black horse, petting his soft coat and distracting herself from the prickle of nerves in her belly. She, Paige, and Alice had surgically deconstructed what to do and say during a horse-drawn carriage ride with Mr. Sea-glass Eyes but their discussion had not prepared her for the real thing—because the sight of Harris standing in front of a pearly white carriage had her organs bouncing around like espresso-guzzling gymnasts. He looked like a real-life prince.

"Can I help you into the carriage?" Harris asked, holding out a gloved hand. His gray wool coat hung open, perfectly comple-menting a chunky cardigan. A plaid scarf draped around his neck, and his coal-black hair was pushed back from his face, tousled in a way that made Gigi's fingers itch to run through it.

"Um, sure." She swallowed and set her mittened hand in his, trying her best to look graceful and casual as she stepped up into the carriage. Hopefully, she managed at least one. "This is so neat." Once aboard, she stood tall, assessing the row of harnessed horses and glittering carriages behind her, all lined up against the snowy curb. When Harris joined her, she turned to face him, but her heart jerked at the sudden close quarters. "Oh, hi," she said, like he'd suddenly appeared from out of nowhere.

"Hey." He returned her awkward greeting with a slightly confused grin.

They were close enough that Gigi could've leaned in and nuzzled her face in his wool scarf. As it was, she got a lungful of whatever his tempting cologne was—dark, woodsy tones mixed with . . . orange peel? Black licorice? It wasn't a familiar scent. Not something that Ryan & Ryan used, but Gigi wondered why they hadn't bottled Harris up. They'd sell out of any product that captured his essence.

Realizing she'd been analyzing his scent for too long, Gigi turned and took a seat on the velvet bench. "I've never done this before," she said, redirecting her thoughts before she asked Harris why he smelled so good.

"I haven't either." Harris eased onto the bench next to her, confirming the carriage was made for two people in love, not two people who worked together. His shoulder and thigh brushed against hers. "Are you okay? Comfortable?" He scooted, trying to give her a little more space.

"Yes, totally fine." Gigi nodded and clasped her hands in her lap, willing her stomach to quit fluttering. Harris wasn't here to give her flutters. They were working, and he was being respectful, putting a few inches between them. Had his scent hypnotized her senseless?

The driver turned, breaking Gigi from her thoughts. "Good evening, Ms. Ricci and Mr. Ryan. I'm Bernard, your driver." He addressed them over his shoulder, the brim of his top hat shadowing his eyes. "Pleasure to have you both aboard this evening. There's a blanket tucked in the leather pocket behind me as well as two thermoses of peppermint hot chocolate. Are you ready to start your tour?"

"Just one minute, please," Gigi replied, digging a few necessities from her coat pockets. "I just need to get my phone set up." Quickly removing her mittens, Gigi attached a flexible phone stand to the carriage and clipped her phone into it. Then she adjusted the setup so her camera would capture her, Harris, and the view of the city street.

Tonight's event was to promote Chicago's Magnificent Mile, a bustling street full of high-end shopping, restaurants, and posh hotels. Each of them was hosting a special one-day Christmas sale, and the sponsoring companies for the Gals' Gift Guide were to promote the sale on social. Gigi had already posted quite a few pictures and reels on the company's social channels, as well as the information on where to purchase SheTime's products during the sale. However, she wanted to finish the evening by live streaming a carriage ride down the picturesque street, highlighting the shopping extravaganza.

"Okay, we're ready, Bernard," Gigi said, starting the live streaming on her phone. Sitting back against the tufted leather, she turned to Harris with a smile. "We're streaming to Christmas music so no one can hear what we say. Just look like you're having a good time." She gave him a big smile, pointing to the edges of her lips for emphasis.

He huffed a puff of steam and returned her smile with one of his own. It looked genuine. "I think I can do that."

As Bernard eased the horse and carriage onto the street, Harris pulled the blanket from the front pocket. "Are you cold?"

Gigi had dressed warm—in wool socks, boots, jeans, a cable-knit sweater, her peacoat, scarf, and beanie—but sitting in thirty-degree weather required an extra layer. "Yes. A little."

He unrolled the plaid blanket and shook it out. "Here." Harris leaned forward, laying it across their legs, letting it bundle against their waists. "Better?"

"Better. Thanks." She grinned, tucking the edge under her rump, appreciating his thoughtful gesture. "But we'll be even warmer with the peppermint hot chocolate." Tipping forward, Gigi grabbed both thermoses and offered one to Harris. He took it and they screwed opened the lids. "Cheers."

"Cheers," Harris replied. They clinked the metal canisters and took slurps of the rich chocolate drink. Gigi sighed and licked her lips as the cocoa warmed her throat, chest, and stomach.

"What a beautiful evening for a carriage ride," Gigi said, taking in their surroundings. Dusk had settled on Chicago's Magnificent Mile, transforming the bustling street into a peaceful winter wonderland. The soft glow of wreath-covered streetlamps cast a golden hue over snow-lined sidewalks. Elegant storefronts illuminated holiday window displays and twinkling lights. Towering skyscrapers reached toward the darkening sky, enclosing them in an unexpectedly quiet cocoon.

"Have you lived in Chicago your whole life?" Harris asked, surprising her with a personal question. Until now, he'd stuck to the topic of business.

Gigi shook her head. "Moved here when I was eighteen. Actually, this is one of the first areas I visited when I got here." Gigi scanned the glittering storefronts, remembering how she'd bopped through stores, mesmerized and blinded, looking through the hopeful, naïve eyes of a girl who'd previously never left the small town she'd grown up in. "Came to Chicago to go to college. Got a full-ride scholarship to Loyola University."

"Impressive. That's a great school." Harris nodded, balancing the thermos on his thigh. "Where'd you grow up?"

"Kansas." Gigi immediately pictured the trailer she, her sister, and mom had called home. Her childhood held both good and tough memories, but as an adult, she recognized how hard her mom had tried. As a single mom, she'd worked long shifts at the diner, doing everything she could to provide for her girls. "Honestly, I didn't really grow up until I moved to Chicago. This city taught me to be independent, even if the lessons were sometimes a little rougher than I would've liked." She gave him a lopsided grin. He returned it.

"The city isn't just a place. It's a process." The words rolled off his tongue, like paint onto a canvas, creating an image Gigi immediately resonated with.

"It is, isn't it?" She marveled at his flippant yet introspective comment. Trial, error, and the city had shaped her into the woman she was today.

"Your family still in Kansas?"

"My mom is. My sister and her husband live in a small town in northern Minnesota—Maple Bay. It's absolutely adorable and I love visiting, but I'm not sure if I could live there."

Harris finished a sip of cocoa. "Why is that?"

She looked ahead, down the lively street. "Chicago has an energy." She pressed her lips together in thought. "Being here fills me up and keeps me going, like the city is a bottomless cup of opportunity, and I just want to drink it up all the time."

"Interesting way to describe it." His expression softened.

She shrugged a shoulder. "Some people need wide-open spaces. I guess I thrive in endless chaos."

He chuckled, like he understood.

"What about you?" she prodded, wondering if Harris would open up. So far, he'd kept his personal life close to his chest—buttoned up like one of his suits. "You must enjoy chaos, too, since you've moved between Chicago and New York City."

He quirked an eyebrow. "Do a little research on me?"

"Isn't it normal to google every new person you meet? I feel like it would be weird if I didn't."

He smirked, seeming to accept her answer. Maybe he'd even done a little research on her? "I guess I've never known any different. Grew up in Chicago and moved to New York City for business, but I think I like the city for a different reason than you do. I appreciate getting lost in the city."

Gigi leaned back against the tufted leather, pondering his response, seeing a crack of light in his wall. "Care to elaborate?"

Harris took another sip from his thermos, staring out over the front of the carriage. He licked his lips before adding, "In a city, there're people everywhere. You're never really alone. Yet, everyone keeps to themselves and lets you be whoever you want to be."

She stared at him, instantly understanding his perspective. "You're surrounded by millions of strangers, but there's also a certain freedom in that."

He glanced at her, as though she'd hit directly on his point. "Exactly."

Gigi smiled softly. "I get that. Being surrounded by a few million people makes me feel like I don't need to fit into a mold. I know there's a place for me here and people who get me. That wasn't always the case where I grew up." He tilted his head, and she continued. "My mom raised my sister and me by herself. She did the best she could, but we were always scraping by, and that somehow separated us from the other kids and families in town. When I graduated high school, I wanted to move somewhere and start fresh. Make my own way."

"You wanted to reinvent yourself? Without the weight of judgements or expectations?" There was a hint of admiration in his tone. It caught her off guard.

"Yeah." Intrigued by his insight, she wondered if he'd done the same. "Is that why you moved to New York City? To reinvent yourself?" This confused her, since Harris had plenty of opportunity laid out for him here in Chicago. Why would he need to start fresh?

"I moved for a business opportunity." He straightened in his seat, not fully answering her question, and Gigi got the feeling she'd hit on something Harris didn't want to talk about. Treading lightly, she moved to a topic he seemed more open on—work.

"You moved there for GambleOnLove?"

He quirked a brow.

"Remember, I googled you," she clarified, instigating a crooked grin from Harris.

"Yes, that's why I moved. I went into business with my best friend, Adam," he replied, and Gigi scrunch her brow. When she'd googled Harris, the articles she'd read noted he was the sole owner of GambleOnLove. Why had he parted from doing business with his best friend? "Our largest investors were in New York City. Ultimately, that's where we opened our office and built a team."

"You're still running that business while working at Ryan & Ryan?" She was pressing for more information, but he simply nodded.

"I like to work."

"Hmm," she replied, clicking her nails on the metal thermos, thinking about his answer, what she knew of Harris, and what she knew of the dating app. She had a million questions, but his last name was on her paycheck. How transparent could she be?

"You look like you have something to say." Harris angled himself toward her.

She huffed, scolding her face. "I've never been good at hiding my thoughts."

"Say it," he replied, plainly, and with a shrug. "I want to hear what your face is saying."

This made her laugh, easing her hesitation, and she went to the first question swirling at the top of the list. "How'd you come up with the idea for the dating app?"

He looked surprised by her question. "The app? It was Adam's idea. He'd always been a 'big picture' thinker. He came up with the idea after a string of bad dates and asked me to partner with him to handle the financials." For a moment, he looked lost in thought. Stuck in a memory? With his next breath, he focused back on her. "That'd never been Adam's forte, and he wanted someone he could trust."

"Hmm," she replied, tapping her lips. "But you obviously believed in the concept of the dating app, in order to commit to it?"

"Yes, of course. I'd never get involved with a business I didn't believe in."

Gigi pursed her lips, trying to keep her inner thoughts from tweaking her face. It didn't work.

"What?" he asked, looking slightly amused. "Do you have something against GambleOnLove?"

"I mean, it is kind of weird, isn't it? To go on a date with someone you don't know and have never seen?"

"It's not really that weird."

"Have you ever done it yourself?"

"Well . . . no," he replied. "That would be a conflict of interest. I'm not going to use an app I helped to create to get a date."

That comment sounded chivalrous, but she still squinted an eye at him. "It just seems like most people use the app for short-term dating, not long-term." This was the nicest way she could think of to avoid calling his app a hookup facilitator.

He shrugged a shoulder, looking like he'd heard this a million times. "There's always going to be a portion of the dating pool that's looking for short-term commitments. That's not specific to a dating app. But GambleOnLove has a sixty-seven percent success rate on matches. Did you know that?"

"Really?" Her eyes widened at this stat. "What do you consider successful?"

"Me? Or the app?" He prodded, throwing her off guard, but not waiting for an answer. "When a couple matches and then starts dating, they put a freeze on their profiles. Our data analysts follow up with our clients every six months, asking for a status of their relationship. Sixty-seven percent of our matches are still dating a year later. Thirty-three percent are married."

"What?" she squeaked, astonished. "A third result in marriage? Really? Are you joking?"

"I wouldn't jest about data," he replied straight-faced, making her grin.

"I just . . ." she started, trying to pinpoint and articulate her issue with the app. "I guess I've always been a little old-fashioned when it comes to dating."

"Old-fashioned? How so?" His focus was fully on her, making her feel like the most interesting thing on the Miracle Mile. Her stomach fluttered again.

"I've always believed in the idea of fate, you know? Like, turning the corner and dumping a full cup of piping hot coffee on the man you were meant to spend the rest of your life with. Or striking up a conversation at a bookstore with a stranger after you both reach for the last copy of the hottest new release. Or—" She pressed her lips together before she mentioned something about tripping out of an elevator and ending up tangled in each other's arms. "There's something romantic about those chance encounters. Plus, I kind of think it's creepy to meet up with some random guy you don't know."

He huffed a laugh, looking entertained. "Who's to say the guy you spill a cup of coffee on is your long-lost love? Maybe fate put him in your path to ruin his shirt because he's been looking for an excuse to buy a new one?"

She frowned, refusing this explanation. "I feel like fate has bigger things to tackle than fashion choices."

Harris cocked his arm, resting it on the side of the carriage. "The thing about dating apps is that they're not about replacing fate or chance. They're about expanding your opportunities to meet new people. It's like casting a wider net into a sea of potential connections. What if you never ran into the potential love of your life simply because he lived on the other side of the city and went to a bookstore close to his apartment to get that hot new release?"

Gigi pursed her lips and countered, "But isn't there something artificial about it?"

Harris nodded, acknowledging her point. "I can understand why you'd think that. But with GambleOnLove, the technology was created to go beyond surface-level judgements. Our algorithm considers a wide range of factors, from personality traits to shared interests and life goals. It's about finding someone who aligns with your values and creating a genuine connection that will go beyond physical appearance. I mean, what if there was a man that could be your best match and you walked by him every day on the way to work but never gave him a second glance because you didn't immediately connect with his physical appearance?"

Gigi's curiosity piqued. After all, she'd definitely picked a few duds simply because her heart had fluttered at a handsome face and a few smooth pickup lines. "I guess that makes sense, but how does the app know if a couple will have chemistry? You know, that spark when you meet someone in person."

"That goes beyond an algorithm. But if a couple doesn't feel the chemistry, they just get back on the app and spin the wheel again, going onto the next match. Technology facilitates the match, but anything beyond that is up to the couple." Harris stretched out his legs, crossing an ankle over the other. "You've never tried a dating app?"

She shook her head. "I don't date much."

"Really?" He looked confused by her response.

"I mean, I'm pretty busy with work and all." Harris's gaze lingered on her, his eyes soft with a hint of something she couldn't quite decipher. A flush rose to her cheeks.

"Interesting," he said, analyzing her. Before she could respond, the carriage came to a halt, jolting Gigi from her thoughts.

"I hope you both enjoyed your time with Windy City Carriage," Bernard said over his shoulder. "Wishing you both a beautiful evening."

Gigi cleared her throat. "Thanks so much, Bernard. It was lovely." She waved and smiled at her phone before ending the live streaming video. As she gathered her phone, Harris tipped Bernard and climbed down from the carriage. Then he took Gigi's hand and helped her down as well. But as she put one boot on the snowy street, she wobbled, slipping on a patch of ice.

Gigi's breath caught in her throat. Before she could brace herself for impact, strong arms wrapped around her, pulling her close—into solid, comforting warmth. Startled, she looked up, finding Harris's steady gaze fixed on her, concern etched on his features.

"Are you alright?" he asked, his voice strung with worry.

Gigi nodded. Her cheeks flushed hot. "I think so," she murmured, grateful he'd caught her. But instead of letting her go, Harris's grip tightened, and before she could protest, he'd scooped her up into his arms, cradling her as though she weighed nothing at all.

"Oh," she breathed, her heart bounding as her boots suddenly dangled far from the ground. Pressed against Harris, she went weak. She molded into his incredibly soft scarf and intoxicating scent. Time stood still as he carried her across the street, like a firefighter saving her from a burning building. She couldn't take her eyes off him.

When Harris finally set her down on the safe, dry sidewalk, Gigi fought the crazy mix of exhilaration and uncertainty which swirled inside her. Her breath hitched as their gazes locked with a silent exchange that spoke volumes.

"Thank you," she managed, her voice barely a whisper.

"Can't have you falling on my watch," he replied easily, but Gigi wondered if she was actually falling . . . for a man she couldn't have.

Chapter Nine

To: gianna.ricci@ryan&ryan.com
From: harrison.ryan@ryan&ryan.com
Re: Spring line packaging

Gigi,

Do you seriously think it's worth spending an extra $3.37 on packaging just to have it look "pretty"? The gold foil and velvet ribbon really cut into our margins for the spring gift sets. I vote we should get rid of the unnecessary frills and increase profitability.

Hanging by a thread,

Harris

*P.S.–I've decided I like the idea of sarcastic signatures.
It eases frustrations in the workday. Please feel free to
match my sarcasm with more of your own.*

To: harrison.ryan@ryan&ryan.com
From: gianna.ricci@ryan&ryan.com
Re: Spring line packaging

Harris,

*I just can't budge on the gold foil and velvet ribbon.
First, they are gorgeous! Second, they give the packaging
a premium look and feel, allowing our products to
stand out on the shelf AND create a memorable "un-*

boxing" experience which holds a lot of value for our customers, especially those purchasing them for gifts.

I'd rather save money by switching out the interior packing material & using the corrugated separators and tissue paper that we already have in inventory.

From the trenches,

Gigi

P.S.–I'm so glad you are joining me in my snarky-ness. You have made my day.

P.S.S.–Rudy is the cutest kitten I've ever seen! He is currently curled in a tiny orange ball on my lap and purring while he dreams. I won't be getting up from my desk until he is done with his nap. I may have to order in lunch.

To: gianna.ricci@ryan&ryan.com
From: harrison.ryan@ryan&ryan.com
Re: Spring line packaging

Gigi,

I'm glad you're seeing the light and willing to change the interior contents. However, I really don't think our target market buys our products for the gold foil and velvet ribbon. Can't we use the black boxes we have in stock? Wouldn't that be sleek? Sophisticated?

Not a single regard,

Harris

P.S.–Rudy is the cutest kitten ever. I agree. You should have seen him last night when he was running around my house like a ninja, attacking a feather that had escaped from a pillow. Completely adorable and en-

tertaining. Also, he really likes crackers, especially with peanut butter. And watching Dateline *with me. Though I Googled if kittens should eat crackers or peanut better and the answer is "no," so I picked up some Kitten Crunch Treats at the pet store. Now, every time I eat a peanut butter cracker, he gets a chicken-cheddar flavored treat.*

To: harrison.ryan@ryan&ryan.com
From: gianna.ricci@ryan&ryan.com
Re: Spring line packaging

Harris,

Black is not on brand for SheTime. Also, please see attached analysis of multiple focus groups over the past few years. Over ninety-five percent of our target market prefers the "pretty" packaging, as you have called it. Saving three dollars is not worth killing our whole spring lineup.

Please see attachment and a therapist,

Gigi

P.S.–Rudy watches Dateline *with you? OMG. I love this! And he loves chicken-cheddar treats? I'm going to stop by the store tonight and get him some so I can keep them in my desk.*

P.S.S.–I might not bring Rudy back to your office until the end of the day. He's too cute and fun. I cannot part with him.

To: gianna.ricci@ryan&ryan.com
From: harrison.ryan@ryan&ryan.com
Re: Spring line packaging

Gigi,

I just spent the last five minutes cleaning my desk because I spit coffee all over it when I read your last signature. So funny. Also, you got me where it hurts—with data. You can keep your pretty packaging. Approved to move forward with the spring gift sets.

Never fast, always furious,

Harris

P.S.–Rudy loves the treats. This has become our midnight snack. I eat crackers. He gobbles up chicken-cheddar treats. Also, he sleeps with me now instead of in his kennel. Does that make me a bad foster parent?

To: harrison.ryan@ryan&ryan.com
From: gianna.ricci@ryan&ryan.com
Re: Spring line packaging

Harris,

First, yesssssss on the packaging! You won't regret it! I promise! Also, who knew you were so funny?? A Fast & Furious reference perfectly morphed into a snarky signature? Touché, Mr. Harris. Touché! You get a gold star today!

Warm regards from the high horse I'm on,

Gigi

P.S.–I'll be stacking my desk with kitten treats. I've also noticed he loves my scarf, so I will knit him one of his own.

P.S.S.–Letting Rudy sleep with you makes you an amazing foster parent. And thank you for sharing your sweet kitten with me.

Chapter Ten

Harris stepped out of the elevator onto the tenth floor, a small grin tugging the corners of his lips upward. He held a paper bag in one hand and a cup of coffee in the other, feeling uncharacteristically lighthearted as he made his way back to his office.

The paper bag contained a mouthwatering chicken salad croissant sandwich and a chocolate chip cookie from the bakery around the corner. But that wasn't what had put a skip in his step. It was the way Gigi had broken into a huge smile when Harris had delivered the same lunch order to her desk.

"For me?" she'd asked, peeking into the brown bag.

"You mentioned you like the chicken salad croissant from Sweet Breads Bakery, and that Rudy was napping, so you couldn't move from your desk."

"You didn't have to do that," she'd said, but her eyes had lit up in appreciation. "But thank you. The croissant sandwich is my *favorite*."

"Consider it a thank you for watching Rudy while I'm in board meetings today." He'd glanced at the purring kitten, lovingly wrapped in a scarf-swaddle on Gigi's lap.

"Anytime." Her smile had widened further.

When Harris returned to his office, he was surprised to find Dean waiting for him, perched on the edge of his desk.

"What're you all smiley about?" Dean asked, as though Harris had just peddled in on a unicycle.

Harris pushed away the blissful memory of Gigi. "Nothing. Just hungry and looking forward to my lunch." He raised the brown bag and piping hot coffee, not wanting to give anything away. He shouldn't be having these thoughts about an employee. He was aware. But the pull to Gigi was getting hard to ignore.

Dean raised an eyebrow, clearly unconvinced. "Come on, spill it," he urged, leaning in closer. "You haven't smiled like that in forever. Did stock in GambleOnLove go up?"

Harris shrugged, irked that Dean would go straight to financial gain, like there was nothing else that could make Harris happy. Then again, he hadn't run across anyone in years that lightened his heart the way Gigi could.

"Yep," Harris replied, and Dean pumped a fist.

"Nice!"

Before Dean could press him further, their father strode into the office. He'd just returned yesterday from a week in Mexico with Karen, apparently eager to get back to work. Harris recognized the folder in his dad's hand as the financial analysis he'd completed on SheTime, before he started working with Gigi and the team.

"I've been reviewing this, and I see your point about dissolving SheTime." Their father slid right into business. No time for greetings. "It would raise our profit margins by fifteen percent overall."

Harris's good mood evaporated at his father's words, replaced by a surprising surge of protectiveness for both Gigi and SheTime. He set his lunch on his desk before replying with, "I might have jumped the gun with my recommendation to dissolve the business."

Dean cocked his head at Harris, as though that was the last thing he'd expected. "Really?"

"You're saying the financials are wrong in here?" Dad raised the papers again.

Harris shook his head. "No, the financials are right." He'd never pull together numbers haphazardly. "But I think we can improve profits with the right strategies. I've started making some changes, working to implement them as quickly as possible."

"That's what I'm talking about," Dean said, giving Harris a brotherly push. "I knew you'd see the light once you started working with Gigi."

Their dad's forehead creased, not as excited about this revelation as Dean was. He shook his head. "Here." He offered the analysis to no one in particular. Harris took it. "You two figure this out together. I don't want to see it again until you've come to a final conclusion about SheTime. These are the kind of hard decisions you'll need to start making without me."

The heavy weight of responsibility settled back on Harris's shoulders. He wasn't planning to stick around. He was here to set Dean up for success. Had Gigi distracted him from his mission? From what was best for his brother? After all, if everything went as planned, Dean would run Ryan & Ryan by himself, and Harris needed to give his brother every advantage possible.

Setting the papers on his desk, Harris said, "We'll have a revised analysis and recommendation to you by Christmas."

By the time Harris and Gigi packed up the booth at the Sip & Shop—an evening gift market and hot cocoa tasting event—they stepped outside to a foot of fresh snow. It blanketed the streets and was still coming down. The usually bustling roads were muffled under a mattress of white. Only the scrape of plows cut through the snowfall and biting wind. Even the tops of the surrounding buildings were barely visible, their outlines blurred by the storm.

"I feel like the morning weatherman completely missed his mark today," Harris said, trying to block Gigi from the wind as she pecked away at her phone, looking for an Uber. His scarf whipped at her, and he stuffed the ends into his coat. "There's a lot more snow than expected. I should've checked on the weather at some point today. Or even stepped outside."

"We were so busy, I didn't even look at my phone until we were packing up." Gigi glanced up at him, her eyes going wide. "The closest Uber is fifty-eight minutes away."

"What?" Harris swiveled, checking their surroundings. The street was desolate. Even the conference hall they'd just left was locking up.

"Maybe there's a restaurant still open? We could get dinner and wait for Ubers?" She covered her eyes, squinting down the street, looking for signs of life.

"Actually, I walked here." Harris grimaced as icy flakes stung the back of his neck. He tugged on his knit hat. The storm was getting worse. "I only live a few blocks from here. Why don't you come to my place? You can wait for an Uber there and I can throw something together for us to eat." The offer hung in the air, laden with both excitement and apprehension. He wanted to spend more time with Gigi but was afraid of where it might lead. Yet there was no other option. He wouldn't leave her here to wait for an Uber that might never come.

When Gigi hesitated, he held his breath, hoping she wouldn't feel uncomfortable or pressured by his invitation. He just wanted to ensure she was safe and warm.

"I'm sure the plows will catch up with the storm in the next few hours and then you'll be able to get an Uber, or I can drive you home," Harris offered. "Plus, I know Rudy would love to see you."

Gigi's apprehension eased. "Okay, that'd be great. I really appreciate it."

He smiled, tugging his scarf further up on his neck. "Follow me."

Harris and Gigi trudged through the snow in silence, focusing on each step and trying not to fall. Though Harris wouldn't mind having a reason to catch Gigi—again. Finally, after what felt much further than a few blocks, they arrived at his brownstone. Harris unlocked the door and ushered Gigi inside, relieved to escape the biting cold.

"We made it," Gigi said on a sigh, unwrapping the scarf that had covered her face like a ski mask.

Harris did the same, bits of ice hitting the floor. "Just barely." He flicked on the light, casting a soft glow in the foyer before setting down the tote bag he'd been carrying for Gigi. "Can I take your coat?"

Gigi shimmied out of her peacoat. She handed it over. "Thank you."

"Welcome to my humble abode." Harris gave their coats a shake and hung them on the iron coatrack to dry.

"Wow, there are never any vacancies in this area. You got really lucky finding this place." Gigi eyed the arched doorways and ornamental tiled ceiling. "It's beautiful."

"Thank you." He grinned. "I actually bought the building about fifteen years ago."

"Building? You own the entire brownstone? All four floors?"

He nodded, tugging off his hat and scarf. "It was an investment. Also, I couldn't bring myself to sell it when I moved. I put a lot of time and effort into the restoration. Plus, I rent out the top two floors."

"Wow," she reiterated. She was clearly impressed, and a surge of pride moved through him. "Well, it's gorgeous. Beautifully decorated." Gigi removed her hat, running a hand through her tousled hair. Her cheeks were rosy red.

"Make yourself at home." He took her hat and scarf, adding them to the coat rack. They both removed their boots, and Harris waved a hand at her. "Come. I'll turn on the fireplace and we can warm up." Leading her through an arched doorway and into the formal sitting room, Harris headed straight for the gas fireplace. He flicked it on, and the room filled with a comforting glow. Gigi gravitated to it like a moth. After clicking on a lamp, Harris joined her, and they soaked up the heat together.

"Marble mantel? Stained glass accent windows? Wingback chairs? Tiffany lamps? My sister would *love* this place." Gigi did a little turn, assessing the room. "She's an interior designer. Super creative and talented."

Harris held his hands out toward the fire. "Sounds like creativity and talent run in the family."

Gigi cocked her head. Her brow creased. "Are you referring to me?"

"Of course." Why did she act like she never got complimented? Was that even possible? "The ideas you come up with for SheTime are so creative. The products, marketing, all the planning and details for events."

She smiled. Softly, like she was allowing his words to sink in. "Thank you."

"You're welcome." Harris was about to expand his compliments, but got distracted by how the flickering flames reflected and danced in Gigi's vibrant eyes. She radiated in the fire's golden glow, her cheeks still tinged with a rosy hue. And when she batted her long eyelashes, a droplet hit her cheek—melting remnants from the storm. It trickled like a tear, and Harris had a strong urge to brush it away. His fingers curled, reacting.

With a nervous laugh, Gigi brushed a hand across her cheek, erasing the droplet and the moment. "I think my eyelashes are unthawing."

Harris chuckled, mostly at himself. What was he doing? "I think we just walked through the storm of the year." His attention went back to the orange flames. "We had a long, but successful day. I think we should celebrate. Are you a wine drinker?"

Her eyes twinkled. "Oh, yes."

"Pinot Noir? Cabernet? Or do you prefer white?"

"Red, white, rose, bubbles. I don't discriminate."

He huffed a laugh. "Perfect. I'll get us a bottle and grab Rudy from my bedroom. Then I can scrounge up some dinner. Though I'm going to apologize in advance. My kitchen was not prepared for company. I'm a little light on options."

Looking excited by this comment, Gigi popped up on her toes and pivoted like a ballerina. "I've got just the thing," she said, walking toward the foyer.

He watched her, confused. "You have something for dinner?"

A few seconds later, Gigi made her way back to him. Her tote bag was slung on her shoulder, and she was digging through it. "I went to the farmer's market this morning, before going to the conference hall. I've got veggies, orzo, chicken bouillon, and a wedge of parmesan." She pulled out a handful of leafy orange carrots, proving her point. "I can make us Italian Penicillin!"

He tipped his head, intrigued and concerned.

"It's my grandma's recipe. Don't worry. It's soup, not medicine." Gigi bounced with a giggle. "But it will definitely make you feel better if you're sick. My grandma makes it for me anytime I'm not feeling well. Can I make it for you? As a thank you for saving me from the storm?"

The wind, sleet, and snow rattled against the front windows and Harris was thankful for the disaster outside. Otherwise, he'd be standing in his kitchen alone, wondering how far past the expiration date his milk was and if he could use it to make mac and cheese. Worse, he'd be wondering all that without Gigi. "Can I be your sous chef? You're a guest at my home. I can't in good conscience have you wait on me."

She shrugged, her eyes bright. "Sounds like a good deal to me."

Harris showed Gigi to the kitchen, which was toward the back of the house, and opened up into his living room. "I'll be back in a minute. Feel free to poke around wherever you like." He jogged upstairs and swooped Rudy out of his kennel, kissing him on his tiny, hairy head. Then he ducked into the library to grab a bottle of his best pinot noir—a bottle he'd picked up a few years back on an impromptu trip to France. He'd been saving it for a special occasion. Being stuck in a snowstorm making soup with Gigi felt like the right time to break it open.

By the time Harris arrived back in the kitchen, Gigi had all the veggies and ingredients splayed across the kitchen island. She'd also found the big wooden cutting board, a knife, and a peeler.

"There's my little cutie pie!" Gigi squeezed her hands to her chest, barely containing her excitement as she rushed over to Harris, going straight for Rudy. For a second, he pictured her greeting him the same way after a long day at work. Ignoring the fleeting thought, Harris offered the meowing kitten, and Gigi cradled him in her arms, like a baby. She scratched his belly, quieting his mews. He raised his white-socked paws to her face.

"I think you might like a little chicken broth," she cooed to Rudy. "I'll warm you up a little bowl after I make the soup. It will warm your tummy."

Harris grinned, leaving the two to snuggle as he opened the wine. "So, tell me about this recipe of yours." He retrieved two wide-bowled pinot noir glasses from a cabinet. "Your grandma taught you how to make it?"

"Yes—my Nonna. That's Italian for grandmother and what I've always called her." She gave Rudy one more squeeze before setting him down. He immediately pounced on one of his catnip toys. The little bell attached to the ball jingled. "We cook together a lot. She's taught me everything I know about Italian food and cooking."

Harris began filling their glasses. "Have you cooked with her since you were a kid?" He pictured Gigi running around her grandma's kitchen in a tiny apron, spreading cheer and a cloud of flour.

"Actually, I didn't meet my Nonna until I was in my twenties."

The image in Harris's head popped. He paused before filling the second glass. "Oh?" he replied, allowing Gigi to expand only if she felt comfortable.

"I think I mentioned in the carriage ride that my mother raised my sister and me by herself." Her words were timid, like she needed to remind him of that conversation, as if he might have forgotten what she'd shared with him. He hadn't. He remembered every word. "I didn't grow up with my dad. He left when I was little. But I'd always been curious about him. My sister and I had some communication with him when we were teenagers and found out he lived in Chicago."

Harris set the wine bottle on the counter. "Is that why you came here?"

She nodded, but hurt flashed across her face. Harris's whole chest tightened, and he wanted to hunt her father down and give him a piece of his mind.

"It is," Gigi confirmed before moving to the kitchen sink. She pushed up her sweater sleeves and washed her hands. When she turned off the faucet, the hurt had dissipated from her beautiful features. "He's why I moved here, but not why I stayed. We don't really talk much anymore."

Harris handed her a glass. "I'm sorry. He's missing out on having an amazing person in his life."

She gave him a grin. "Thank you. He is. But, in moving here and trying to connect with him, I got to meet my Nonna, and she embraced me and my sister with open arms. She's amazing and I'm grateful to have her in my life. We actually live in the same apartment building. I see her just about every day. She loves my friends, too, and spoils us all with her cooking. I'm blessed to have her in my life."

"She sounds like a gem." Harris raised his glass. "Cheers to Nonna?"

Gigi brightened. She clinked his glass. "Cheers to Nonna."

They both sipped, keeping steady eye contact over the thin glass rims.

Lowering her glass, Gigi smacked her lips together. Then she ran the tip of her tongue over her top lip. "That is delish!"

Harris's pulse quickened. He almost forgot he was drinking wine. "I'm glad you like it."

Gigi took another sip before setting her glass on the island. "Okay, let's make some soup." She put herself in front of the cutting board and picked up a carrot.

"What else can I get you?" Harris asked, as Gigi began peeling the vegetable.

"Do you have salt?" Her brow quirked at this. "Because I peeked in your fridge and I'm kind of amazed you even survive. Do you live on sparkling water and beef jerky sticks?"

"I'm a take-out afficionado," he countered. "But, yes, I have salt. I'm not a heathen."

"Good. I'm glad you're not a heathen." She winked, and he grinned. "I need salt, two large pots, a blender, and a cheese grater."

As Gigi prepped the vegetables and Rudy pranced through the kitchen, Harris gathered her list. At her instruction, he also added water and chicken bouillon to one pot and set it on the stove, turning the gas burner to medium heat. By the time he was done, she'd chopped the carrots, garlic, and onion. Next, she took hold of the celery, slicing it with the gusto of a Michelin Star chef.

Harris leaned against the counter, watching her in awe. "I'd take off my finger if I tried to chop that fast."

"No, you wouldn't. It just takes practice."

"I don't know. That looks like talent to me." Harris leaned in over the island to watch Gigi maneuver the knife with precision. Her easy movements nearly hypnotized him.

"Here, let me show you," she said, reaching for him.

Before he knew it, Gigi had tugged him close. She placed the knife in his hand and slid her delicate fingers over his. As she did, Harris molded his body around her, angling himself to watch over her shoulder. The warmth of her touch sent a sizzle down his spine, and Harris focused hard, reminding himself that he had hold of a sharp blade.

Keep yourself in check. Harris repeated the warning in his head, but his body was screaming the opposite.

"Put the tip of the knife on the board and move the blade up and down, using the tip as a lever." Gigi guided Harris's hand, and they completed a few slices together. "Always cut using the center of your blade." They chopped a few more times, her sweet, sugar-cookie scent dislodging every thought from his brain. "See, it's so easy. You got this." Gigi turned her head, smiling proudly and placing her lips just inches from his. Their gazes locked and Harris's heart lurched, like it wanted to jump out of his chest and join the veggies on the cutting board.

Without thinking, his hand moved to her waist, to ground himself. At his touch, Gigi's blush lips parted, as if she were inviting him to kiss her. In that instant, Harris knew he was a goner. He was being drawn to her like a magnet.

"You got this," she repeated, barely over a whisper, and with her next breath, Harris swore she leaned into him. He was exercising excessive discipline to keep from closing the distance, which felt like an inch and a mile at the same time. Every fiber of his being was screaming to give into temptation, to let go of all the reasons he shouldn't, and just kiss her.

Chapter Eleven

Gigi couldn't pinpoint what spurred her decision to pull Harris close—there were too many reasons. Maybe it was his genuine interest in what made her tick. Or his caring nature that surfaced in the form of chicken-salad croissants and saving kittens. Perhaps it was how he always seemed to catch her whenever she stumbled. Or maybe it was simply the idea of being wrapped up in his strong arms and intoxicating scent.

All Gigi knew was that she couldn't resist any longer. He'd shown her the real Harris—the man behind his stern exterior. And she wanted that man to kiss her.

Staring into his sea-glass eyes, catching the blues and greens that melded together, she was certain his appreciative gaze held the same unmet desire that crackled through her. Her body temperature was rising at record speed. Soon she'd need to fan herself.

But instead of leaning in and instigating her fantasy, Harris did the opposite. He grimaced and took a step back. The warmth of his hand disappeared from her waist, and disappointment washed over her in a wave, mingling with embarrassment.

"I—" she started, putting a hand on the counter to stabilize herself. She wanted to explain away the last few seconds, but Harris didn't let her backpedal.

He crouched down quickly, capturing a rambunctious Rudy—who was climbing up Harris's pant leg like Spiderman. "Ouch!" Harris gently peeled the kitten from his leg and held him up between the two of them. His orange ears flattened as though his evil plan was ruined.

Oh. The kitten. The grimace wasn't meant for her. *Thank God.*

"You feisty little thing." Gigi's voice came out strained and a little too bright.

"Jealous cause we weren't paying attention to you?" Harris asked the kitten, and Gigi forced a smile. She was thankful he'd stepped back because of cat claws, not because of her. Still, there was a palpable awkwardness now hanging in the air.

What had just happened? Would Harris have kissed her if Rudy hadn't innocently interrupted? Or was she misreading him?

Regardless, the spell was broken. The moment lost. The warmth of Harris's touch faded as quickly as it had come.

Wanting to erase the awkwardness, Gigi turned and went back to chopping the celery. "Almost done here." She sang her words. "What's the status on the broth?"

Harris cleared his throat and stepped over to the stove. "It's simmering," he replied, like they hadn't just devoured each other with their eyes. Gigi took that as a cue.

"Perfect timing," she said, referring to the broth, not the rampant feelings brewing inside her. Picking up the cutting board, she carried it to the pot and swiped in all the veggies. Then she added a dash of salt, put on the lid, and took a hefty sip of her wine.

"Can you point me to your bathroom?" She needed a few minutes to pull herself together.

"Just down the hall. First door on the right," Harris replied, and Gigi retreated. Once she was behind a closed door, she yanked her phone from her pocket and immediately tapped out an SOS to her friends.

> Gigi: I almost just kissed my boss.

In a matter of seconds, Paige and Alice came to her rescue.

> Paige: I have so many questions. How did you ALMOST kiss your boss?

> Alice: We need to FaceTime you...now!

> Gigi: I can't! I'm in his bathroom...

> Paige: Again...SO MANY QUESTIONS!

Alice: In his bathroom? Like at his house??

Gigi: I couldn't get an Uber. His place was a few blocks from the event. Now I'm snowed in at my boss's house and we're making Nonna's Italian Penicillin.

Alice: OMG! You're cooking together and watching the snow fall? No wonder you almost kissed!

Paige: Did you WANT him to kiss you??

Gigi's fingers itched to respond with "yes!" immediately. She clenched them into a fist at the impulse.

Gigi: I think so. I don't know. I mean . . . yes. But that's crazy, right? He's my boss. I can't just go around kissing him! That's such a bad idea . . . right? Someone tell me what to do!

Paige: Hmmm . . . I thought he was a grumpy grinch that was blowing up your life and didn't understand women? If so, please don't kiss him.

Gigi: I've gotten to know him better. He's actually really sweet. And funny.

Plus, he's dreamy, thoughtful, sexy, and has gotten his life together, Gigi thought, glancing around his guest bathroom. A fluffy hand towel was perfectly folded and hung. Charcoal-gray soap and lotion bottles complemented the accent tiles in the waterfall shower behind her. Reaching out, Gigi pulled open a sink drawer, searching for anything that would expose Harris's downfalls. Instead, she found a tidy organization of miniature toiletries for guests.

Gigi froze, staring at the selection of toothpaste tubes and shampoos. Her last boyfriend's bathroom had housed stinky towels and random, unmatched socks. Harris was a grown man with his life figured out.

Paige: Are you sure? The last few guys you dated were jerks. I don't trust your man-radar. We need to meet him before you kiss him.

Alice: Kiss him . . . PLEASE! I want to hear all the details at Yappy Hour! You're snowed in with Mr. Sea-Glass Eyes. Live your life! Somebody needs to! I'm watching reruns of *Golden Girls* and knitting a cat toy for Tux.

Gigi: You're right.

Paige: Me or Alice?!

Alice: Get to kissing!!

Gigi: I don't have the best guy-radar, and I've been in his bathroom for way too long! Better get going.

Paige: Keep us updated!

> Alice: Kiss him, PLEASE!

With a sigh, Gigi stuffed her phone back in her pocket, unsure if she wanted to wrap herself around Harris or run out into the snowstorm. Paige's comments reminded Gigi of her last relationship, and the disaster that had been. She'd been in love—or so she thought—with Keith. That was until he'd broken up with her on Valentine's Day, leaving her alone at a fancy restaurant, amongst a sea of gushy couples. He'd also left her with the bill, after taking his meal to go.

He was a jerk. And she'd thought she loved that jerk.

In hindsight, she'd always made excuses for Keith. In their three-year relationship, they'd broken up twice, and he'd wormed his way back into her life with smooth words that never aligned with his actions. He'd stolen her time when it was convenient for him, and she didn't see that until he broke her heart for the last time.

But that's what love did, right? It blinded people to pitfalls. And Gigi wanted to see clearly. She couldn't get wrapped up in some fantasy. Who was she kidding? She didn't know Harris well enough to chance heartbreak. Or worse. She couldn't risk the turmoil in her workplace. He was her boss. No matter how much she liked him . . .

There would be NO KISSING.

After walking back into the kitchen, Gigi went to the gorgeous, six-burner gas stovetop and stirred the fragrant, simmering soup. She turned the burner down to low and was going to clean up, but Harris had beat her to it. He'd washed the cutting board and knives. The island was wiped down.

"Want to watch a movie?" Harris stood between a lush beige couch and an ottoman, remote in hand. The massive TV, which hung on the wall, flickered as he clicked past news and commercials, hesitating when "White Christmas" streamed through the speakers. On the screen, Michael Bublé crooned into a microphone, backed by a band and stage.

Gigi's heart raced at the thought of snuggling up on the couch with Harris, enjoying the Christmas special or watching a movie, but she quickly pushed the thought aside. Wanting to avoid another Harris-trance, she suggested the first thing that came to mind. "Actually, I was thinking we could decorate your house."

He glanced at her, raising his eyebrows. "Decorate?"

"Yeah, you know, add a little Christmas cheer to your place," Gigi replied, trying to sound casual. The soup needed an hour to simmer, and Gigi wanted something to do. Curling up on the couch with Harris sounded like the gateway drug to everything she was trying to avoid. "You've been so busy, you haven't had time to get a tree or decorate. I can help with that." His house was pristine, but Gigi had yet to discover a single holiday bauble. Maybe Harris hadn't brought any decorations from his place in New York?

"I don't usually decorate for Christmas," Harris admitted. Muted TV light flickered across his face.

"What do you mean?" Gigi blinked at him, not understanding. Her apartment had been blasted with Christmas since the weekend after Thanksgiving. She looked forward to hauling out her red and green totes every year, which were filled to the brim with décor.

"It's just me. I don't really see the point in decorating."

"Nonsense." Gigi waved a hand at him. "Christmas makes everything better. Even if you're the only one to enjoy it." She sensed his hesitation, but pushed forward, determined to bring holiday cheer into his house and life. "Come on. You've got to have some decorations, right?"

He rubbed the back of his neck. "I guess I probably have a few things packed away."

"Great!" Gigi clapped her hands together. "Point me in the direction!"

They made their way to a closet off the front hall, where Harris removed a few totes before pulling out a small, dusty cardboard box from the back of the closet.

"I don't have much," he warned as they walked back to the living room. He set the box on the ottoman, and Rudy bounced over to sniff as Harris opened the folded cardboard flaps.

Gigi peered inside, finding a few worn decorations—some tinsel, a string of lights, and a handful of ornaments. He wasn't kidding when he said he didn't have much.

"That's perfect." She smiled, pulling out a tangled bundle of lights. "We'll make it work."

Gigi walked over to the kitchen island, zoning in on an outlet on the side. As soon as she plugged in the string of lights, the colorful bulbs illuminated her hands. "Great! All the bulbs are still good!

Now we just need to untangle them." Setting the ball of lights on the island, Gigi tugged away, loosening the knot.

Harris joined her, plucking away as well. "I haven't seen these in a long time."

The lights looked old. Vintage. Gigi was surprised the bulbs still worked. "The multi-colored lights are my favorite. They just feel cozier than white, you know? It's something about the tones."

He smiled softly at her. "Yeah, I like them the best too."

Between the two of them, the tight ball started to loosen, expanding into a mess of wire on the island.

Gigi bent over to get a better look at a stubborn knot. "What was your favorite gift you've ever gotten for Christmas?" she asked, trying to keep the conversation light.

Harris was quiet for a few beats, his fingers working on the green wire. "My favorite?"

"Yeah. What was your favorite, and why?"

"Probably a Lego set I got when I was twelve years old," he replied, his voice tinged with nostalgia. It was enough to drag Gigi's stare up. She caught the memory in his eyes. "It was a massive pirate ship. My brother and I had been begging for it all year."

She smiled, picturing a young Harris eagerly tearing open the gift on Christmas morning.

"It took us an entire weekend to put it together," he continued. "Our mom helped, too, in between making us peppermint hot chocolate, sugar cookies, and actual sustenance to fuel our work."

Her grin widened. "That's a very sweet memory."

"It is." Harris nodded, his gaze going back to the lights. "How about you? Do you have a favorite gift?"

Gigi threaded the lights through a loop, untying a major knot. "It's similar to yours." She spread the loose strand on the island before starting on the next cluster. "My sister and I got a beautiful dollhouse. It was secondhand from a thrift store in town, but to us, it was a dream house. We spent hours making up stories about the lives our dolls lived in that house. But mostly, it was my favorite gift because of the many memories made with my sister."

"I love that." Red, green, and yellow lights reflected across Harris's fingers and sweater. They sparkled in his unguarded eyes.

"It's not the gifts that make the season special, right?" she added. "It's the time spent, and memories made with family and friends. That's what makes Christmas special."

"I agree." Harris shifted his stance before tackling the last bundle. When that was undone, they spread the string of lights over the island.

"Where should we put these?" he asked.

"It's a longer strand than I thought." Gigi tapped her chin before completing a spin to check out the options. "How about we hang them around those windows?" She pointed past the couch. "We can drape them on the curtain rod."

"I like it." Harris unplugged the lights and gathered them into his arms.

"We could hang your ornaments from the lights too!" Gigi's voice lifted with excitement at the idea. "That would be perfect!" She walked over to the ottoman and peered into the box, counting the ornaments. There were five—just enough to add some extra sparkle to the lights.

Harris joined her as she pulled out a snow globe. She gave it a gentle shake, and white flakes swirled around a miniature family building a snowman. The globe hung from a red velvet ribbon, and a string of white music notes were painted on the matching red base.

"This is beautiful," Gigi breathed, admiring the delicate ornament as she turned it over in her hands, finding a tiny gold crank on the bottom. "Does it play music?"

"It used to." Harris cleared his throat, moving the bundle of lights from one arm to the other. "It's been broken since I was a kid, but it was my mom's favorite ornament. I honestly can't remember the song it used to play, but I vividly remember my mom winding it up each year when we decorated the tree. She'd dance with us boys while it played." His voice was thick with emotion and Gigi studied his face, trying to decipher his reaction. She knew his father was remarried, but knew nothing of Harris and Dean's mother.

"That's really sweet. The globe holds special memories for you," she concluded, before holding her tongue, giving Harris space to open up further if he wanted to.

"It does." He caught her gaze. His thumb moved back and forth over the bundle of lights, like it was a worry stone. "My mother passed away when I was twelve. The Christmas we built the Lego ship was my last Christmas with her."

Gigi sucked in a breath. Her heart sunk, and she set a hand on his arm. "I'm so sorry. I didn't know."

A sad smile hitched one side of his lips. "That's why I'm not a huge fan of Christmas. It was never the same without her."

Her fingers slid down his arm, over his sweater, past the collection of bulbs and wire. She found his hand and clenched it, offering silent support for the tragedy he'd endured and the memories he held dear. The gesture eased the pain in his eyes. "I'm sorry. I shouldn't have pushed you to decorate."

"It's okay. You didn't know," he allowed, squeezing her hand back. "This is honestly the first Christmas I've enjoyed in a long time. Thanks for reminding me that there's still happiness to be found in this season." His sad smile went soft and genuine, stealing breath from Gigi's lungs.

"Me?" she asked. Her heart wobbled. "I reminded you of that?"

Harris held her gaze, gratitude shining in his eyes. In that moment, Gigi felt their connection deepen, going beyond work and responsibilities. This vulnerable side of him, this raw honesty about his past, tugged at her heartstrings in a way she couldn't ignore.

"Yes, you did," he confirmed. "Your enthusiasm for Christmas, your persistence to get me involved in the activities, your willingness to share memories . . ." He shrugged. "It brought a lightness to my heart that I haven't felt in a long time."

Gigi's cheeks flushed. She hadn't expected her love of the holidays to affect him so deeply, especially since she'd initially forced it on him to make him uncomfortable. But it had done the opposite—it had eased his pain.

And now, all she wanted to do was douse him in Christmas cheer. To make him smile and laugh. To help him love the season all over again—just like she did.

"We need to put your mother's ornament in a very special place." Gigi held the snow globe delicately, wanting to honor the memory of the woman Harris loved and missed. "It needs to be seen and appreciated every single day."

Chapter Twelve

Harris looked up from his spot, nestled in the couch's corner. It was past midnight, the living room softly illuminated by the television and string of lights that framed his windows. The lights fell in swoops, draped and secured on the curtain rod. He and Gigi had hung them together, using a stepladder, zip ties, and plenty of laughter. The ornaments were perfectly spaced out, dangling at the low point of each drape, and his mom's snow globe took center stage, casting a warm, nostalgic net over the room.

Harris had to admit, the decorations were both beautiful and comforting, and the woman who slept beside him had orchestrated it all, with her touches and presence. Gigi lay stretched out on the couch, her mahogany hair piled on top of her head in a messy, adorable bun. She was half-covered by a blanket Harris had carefully tucked around her.

Earlier, after enjoying bowls of the hearty, rich soup Harris couldn't get enough of, they had laughed through *Home Alone* and nearly made it through *Elf* before Gigi's eyes fluttered shut during the last scene. Now she clung to a pillow, breathing deeply. Harris didn't want to move and wake her, especially since she'd tucked her toes under his thigh.

Instead, he lay his head back, resting it against the cushions to enjoy the view. Beside him, Rudy was curled into an orange ball and settled into the crook of his elbow.

"Do you think I should wake her?" he whispered to Rudy, slowly petting his tiny head. Rudy purred, never opening his eyes. "She's going to get a crick in her neck if we let her sleep there all night." Cause she certainly wasn't going home. Harris had been watching the weather, and the storm wasn't supposed to let up until the morning.

Continuing to pet Rudy, Harris's gaze shifted between Gigi's peaceful face and the strand of twinkling lights. Was this what it was like to have someone to care for and come home to? To have someone to look forward to? Could this be his every day? It couldn't be that easy.

The thought unsettled him, stirring up emotions he wasn't sure how to process. For so long, he'd buried himself in his work, convinced he didn't need anyone else to be happy. His previous girlfriends had all come to the same conclusion—that he was un-available and unworthy of their time. He couldn't commit. And maybe they were right. He had never put them first. But he'd also never met someone like Gigi—someone that deserved a man's full heart.

But love could be painful.

Harris knew too well the ache of losing loved ones. His mother wasn't the only important person taken from him. He'd lost his best friend Adam too. Life was tough, unpredictable. It could be unexpectant in the worst way. But work was always there for him, ready to fill every minute and thought. Had it become his shield? His way of keeping love and eventual heartbreak at bay?

Harris rubbed the back of his neck, inner turmoil running rampant. After tonight, he couldn't deny the feelings that had been lurking and growing since he'd met Gigi. He hadn't realized how lonely he was until she burst into his life, filling it with joy he'd either been avoiding or hadn't known existed.

He looked at her now, peacefully asleep, her presence a balm to his hardened soul. Could he be the man she deserved?

As much as Harris knew he could fall in love with Gigi, a big part of him feared he wasn't capable. He was too firmly set in his ways, too focused on his work to make room for someone else. And Gigi deserved an all-encompassing love.

With a heavy heart, Harris sighed, the weight of uncertainty pressing on him. But one thing was certain: through all his travels and all the money he'd made, he'd never truly known what it meant to have a room with a view—not until tonight.

Reaching out, he put a hand on her leg, waking her with a gentle shake. "Gigi? Can I show you to the guest room?"

Chapter Thirteen

To: harrison.ryan@ryan&ryan.com
From: gianna.ricci@ryan&ryan.com
Re: Today's Meeting with Fragrance Fusions

Harris,

I've NEVER seen that guy crumble like he did today. Seriously?! A twenty percent reduction in cost for all our spring fragrances? A new contract negotiated and signed in a matter of hours? I'm dead. That vendor has been completely holding out on me! That's going to make a huge difference in our margins for the spring product line. Thanks for being super grumpy and extra scary! I especially liked it when you told him "over my dead body" and he choked on his coffee.

Sincerely amused,

Gigi

ell

To: gianna.ricci@ryan&ryan.com
From: harrison.ryan@ryan&ryan.com
Re: Today's Meeting with Fragrance Fusions

Gigi,

First of all, that sales rep is a pompous prick. He rubbed me the wrong way when he referred to you as "darling" at the start of our meeting. That's completely inappropriate in a professional setting, and I saw the way you squinted when he said it. It rubbed you the wrong way too. Not appropriate. He deserved all my snark and nasty stares.

By the way, we make a good team in the boardroom. Dare I say that was the best rendition of "good cop, bad cop" I've ever been a part of? Yes, I dare to say it. We squeezed every last drop out of that guy. He didn't even see it coming.

Regards to the edge of my patience,

Harris

To: *harrison.ryan@ryan&ryan.com*
From: *gianna.ricci@ryan&ryan.com*
Re: *Today's Meeting with Fragrance Fusions*

Harris,

We gave Starsky and Hutch a run for their money! I'm on an adrenaline high . . . or I might have had one too many cups of coffee this morning. Either way, I'm feeling good and excited about the progress today. What other vendors can we bring in to talk about cost savings?

Slightly going off the rails,

Gigi

To: gianna.ricci@ryan&ryan.com
From: harrison.ryan@ryan&ryan.com
Re: Today's Meeting with Fragrance Fusions

Gigi,

I've got a list. But first, I think we should celebrate our win today. Dinner on the company? Are you a seafood fan? Steak? There's a restaurant a few blocks from the office with a killer shrimp cocktail and rib-eye. Plus, their dessert menu is to die for.

Counting down the minutes to happy hour,

Harris

———*ele*———

To: harrison.ryan@ryan&ryan.com
From: gianna.ricci@ryan&ryan.com
Re: Today's Meeting with Fragrance Fusions

Harris,

I'm in! You had me at "dessert menu."

Tiramisu is my spirit animal,

Gigi

"You ordered how many desserts?" Nonna asked, her brow lifting to her silver hairline. She stood in front of the stove, stirring a pot of simmering marinara. It was Friday night Yappy Hour at Gigi's apartment. Christmas music played softly in the background. Gigi was at the kitchen counter, assembling homemade ravioli. Alice and Paige lingered close, margaritas in hand, their knitting projects abandoned in the living room.

"Seven," Gigi confirmed, adding fresh, chopped basil to the mixing bowl full of ricotta, mascarpone, parmesan, and egg. She smiled, recalling the table for two that'd been overflowing with sweet masterpieces. "I told Harris I couldn't choose between the tiramisu and the crème brûlée, so he ordered one of every dessert on the menu. We had a few bites of each, and he sent all the leftovers home with me so we could finish them tonight."

"I like him already." Nonna gave a swift, approving nod.

Alice sighed with her whole chest. "That's so sweet."

Paige—ever the skeptic—leaned back against the counter and tilted her head. "I'm not approving until we get to meet him. Sorry. I said what I said." She sipped her drink and popped her lips. "He's not winning me over with desserts, no matter how good they are.

I need to judge this man for myself. He needs to be worthy of you. You are an absolute catch, and he better know that."

Gigi picked up the mixing bowl and cradled it in her arm. "He's not—" She took hold of the spatula and started stirring, images of Harris rolling through her mind. For a second, she forgot her point. Because she couldn't think of what Harris wasn't. He checked so many of her boxes. "He's my boss."

"I think that's an excuse," Alice said, calling Gigi out. "I think you're letting a certain bad relationship sour you to the potential of something good."

Gigi grimaced. "It was a *really* bad relationship," she replied, referring to Keith. Gigi didn't have to say his name. Her friends and Nonna knew exactly who she was referring to.

"Uck, Keith," Nonna added, like she'd just eaten moldy bread. "I never liked him."

"I know. I should have listened to you from the start." Gigi stirred with extra vigor, vowing never to date anyone her nonna didn't love.

"He-who-should-not-be-named was the absolute worst," Paige interjected, crossing her arms and balancing her margarita in the crook of her elbow. "Remember when Alice and I ran into him at the grocery store after he broke up with you the second time? I literally threw a squash at his head."

"And then I told the manager he was stealing bananas." Alice crossed her arms, mimicking Paige as if they were Gigi's body-guards.

Gigi chuckled. "I wish I had seen that firsthand."

"We do too," Paige and Alice replied together.

Gigi smiled gratefully at her friends. "You guys are the best friends I could ever ask for."

"You'd do it for us." Paige shrugged.

"Absolutely, I would," Gigi replied.

"True friends throw squash at people that hurt their friends. I wish I would've tossed a watermelon at him." Paige looked like she was considering additional fruit arsenal options.

Alice laughed and coughed through a margarita sip.

"If I ever see that guy again, I'll trip him with my cane." Nonna scrunched her face, disgusted with the thought of seeing him.

Gigi grinned at her. "For everyone's sake, let's hope there are no run-ins with him ever again."

Nonna nodded in agreement before tasting the red sauce with a spoon. She made a face of approval—for the sauce—before she said, "Enough talk of history that won't be repeated. Gianna, my love. Do you like this man—this Harris—or not? Because life is short. There's no time for wishy-washiness."

Gigi stopped stirring. She held tight to the spatula, as if it were a stake in the ground. Paige and Alice stared at her, awaiting a response, and Gigi chewed her bottom lip until she might've made it bleed. Then she gave in. "Okay, I like him."

Allison squealed and hopped in place. Margarita sloshed out of her glass to the floor. "I knew it! I knew it! Yay!"

Paige didn't squeal, but after a few beats, her face softened. Gigi could practically see the gears turning in her head. She was compiling a million interview questions to drill Harris if she had a chance to meet him.

Nonna gave a concise nod, approving of Gigi's quick decision-making. "Then you need to make that known to him," Nonna started. "No more wasting time. If you know you like him, then you do something about that." She added a pinch of salt to the sauce, as though she'd solved all of Gigi's problems and she was moving on to the next task.

Gigi sighed in exasperation. Paige and Alice had been hounding her about Harris since the almost-kiss and the overnight stay during the snowstorm, but Gigi didn't have any solid answers. There were too many variables. "I can't just pursue my boss. It's not that easy. It's crazy, actually."

Nonna waved her hand dismissively. "What's the worst-case scenario?"

"I lose my job," Gigi blurted.

"So, you get a new one."

"It's not that easy."

"Love is not easy. It's not easy to find and not easy to keep." Nonna turned, making eye contact with Gigi, Paige, and then Alice, ensuring her point was clear. "I would do anything for one more day with my Alfonso." Her words dropped like a hammer on the tile floor, cracking through Gigi's defenses.

She grimaced before reaching out and putting a hand on her Nonna's arm. "I know."

Gigi's biological grandfather passed before she'd moved to Chicago. She hadn't gotten the chance to meet him, but felt like she'd knew him through all the stories Nonna told her. To Gigi, that was her example of true love—her nonna and papa—hand in hand to the very end, together through every bump, bruise, and laugh.

Nonna patted Gigi's hand and smiled. "Cheer up. I don't say that to make you sad. I had fifty years of a great love. I am beyond blessed. What I mean is that you shouldn't be dilly-dallying around if the potential of a great love is staring you in the face. Either move forward or move on. Enjoy life. Enjoy all those that love you." Nonna squeezed Gigi's hand before glancing at Alice and Paige. "That goes for all of you. Don't waste your precious time with anyone that doesn't show you love. Okay?"

Gigi swallowed, processing Nonna's advice. "Okay," she replied. Paige and Alice agreed as well.

"Good," Nonna said, her tone firm but gentle. "Now, finish those raviolis. This sauce is almost at perfection." She winked, and Gigi went back to the counter. Alice and Paige joined her to help assemble dinner, and as each dollop of filling was spooned onto the sheets of pasta, Gigi's mind got clearer. *No more dilly-dallying*, she determined.

Chapter Fourteen

Harris zipped up his coat, tugging the collar tight against the biting wind. He and Gigi had just wrapped up a Gift Guide event, an evening with Santa and Mrs. Claus. Excited children had their pictures taken while sponsoring companies handed out door prizes and grab bags. As they left the lively venue, snowflakes swirled around them. The streets were festive, adorned with twinkling lights and holiday decorations, but it was Gigi who held his gaze. He wasn't ready for the night to end, and his breath hitched when she brushed her arm against his, giving him a playful nudge.

"There's this great bar nearby that has a really fun trivia night. Want to go for a drink?" she suggested, her eyes sparkling.

Harris smiled at the invitation, trying not to look like the Cheshire cat. "Do they have nachos?" He didn't care if the bar served raw broccoli and Brussels sprouts.

"*Amazing* nachos. Slathered in cheese."

"Count me in."

They walked through the snow to a bar on the corner of the block, a neon sign flickering through a frosted window. Inside, the atmosphere was lively and casual, with groups of friends huddled around wooden tables, laughter and chatter humming through the air. A long, polished bar stretched along one side, lined with high stools. Behind it, there was an extensive array of colorful, shelved bottles.

"Oh, good," Gigi said, leading him to a table in the corner. "Trivia hasn't started yet."

As they shed layers, the server took their drink orders, and Gigi also asked for an order of loaded nachos. When the host's voice came over the speakers, announcing that the first trivia round would start shortly, Gigi's eyes gleamed with excitement.

"I've got the app on my phone. We can play together." The enthusiasm in her voice was infectious, as she searched for her phone in her purse.

Harris grinned as they settled into chairs. "You a regular here?"

"Alice, Paige, and I have been a few times," Gigi admitted, finding her phone and setting it on the table. "They have some great prizes. Last time I won a bread maker."

"A bread maker?" Harris echoed, his eyebrows lifting, not sure if she was kidding.

"Yeah, a really good one. All the bells and whistles. Makes a mean sourdough. I love it." She laughed, making Harris chuckle.

"Hopefully, we can top the bread maker tonight. Maybe a Crock-Pot?"

"Amazing. I need a new one," she replied, and they shared a smile. The warmth between them was almost tangible. He wanted to scoop it up into his arms.

A few minutes later, the server delivered their drinks—hot toddies in glass mugs, each topped with a lemon slice and cinnamon stick. As they slurped warm sips, the host's voice came over the speakers again. He explained the rules, and Gigi slid her chair around the table, scooching close to Harris. She held her phone up in front of him, showing him the trivia app.

"The faster we pick an answer, the more points we get, as long as it's correct," she explained. But Harris was more focused on how close she was. And how much closer he wanted her to be.

"Then I better make sure I can see." He tugged her chair toward him. Gigi's eyes widened, but she quickly relaxed, letting her knee fall against his thigh. A hot rush spread through him, mimicking his swallow of hot toddy.

"You any good at trivia?" She stared at him through thick lashes, as though he better say yes.

"Depends on the topic." He tapped his fingertips on the table. Gigi's proximity and playful gaze had his full attention. It had put him on edge, but in the best way possible.

She pursed her lips, like she had something to say, but kept her thoughts to herself when the start of the game was announced.

Gigi raised her phone, and they both leaned in, waiting for the first question to appear. Harris was determined to impress her, so when the question popped up on the screen, he was beyond excited for a topic he knew well. He didn't need to consider the multiple-choice answers.

Over the speakers, the host also read the question to the bar. "What was the title of the first novel written by Jane Austen?"

"*Sense and Sensibility*," Harris and Gigi said at the same time, and Gigi immediately tapped the answer on her phone. They locked eyes. Gigi's mouth popped open in what Harris hoped was awe.

"Are you a reader?" she asked. Harris nodded.

"I love to read," he replied. "Nothing like getting lost in a good book." Though staring into Gigi's rich, chocolate eyes had him doubting his comment.

"What's your favorite book?"

He grimaced, sitting back in his chair. "That's an impossible question."

"It's an *interesting* question. The answer reveals a lot about a person," she challenged. "You can only pick one. You're stranded on a deserted island and only have one book to read. What is it? Tell me. Don't think too hard about it. What's the first one that comes to mind?"

"On a deserted island?"

She nodded.

"Probably *Survival for Dummies*."

Gigi squinted, looking entertained by his sarcasm. "No, really. What would it be?"

"*The Great Gatsby*. F. Scott Fitzgerald."

She tipped her head, her silky hair falling to one shoulder. "Interesting."

"How so?"

"Why is it your favorite?" She was analyzing him in ways he wished he could put words to. Before he could respond, she added, "For its exploration of the American dream and unrequited love?"

Harris froze, locking in on her, immediately wanting to pick her brain about the story and its themes. Was that the hottest thing he'd ever heard? "Yes," he uttered. It was the only word he got out.

Gigi tapped her chin and pursed her lips, looking thoughtful. "Very interesting."

"It's also my favorite because of the themes of love and loss. The exploration of the illusion of success. The complex characters and relationships. It's poetic and symbolic. I get something new out of the story every time I read it."

She bit her fingernail, looking intrigued by his comments. "That's because you've lived more life every time you reread it. You've grown. The story resonates differently at different times of your life."

"So true," he said, captivated by her insights.

"I always thought the love story in *The Great Gatsby* was so haunting. Gatsby's obsession with Daisy, the lengths he goes to for her . . . it's heartbreaking." Her fingers brushed his hand, ever so briefly, forcing something low in his stomach to melt.

"It is," Harris agreed. "But it's not just about their love. It's also about how Gatsby's idealized vision of Daisy and the past ruins him."

Gigi sighed softly, her eyes flickering with understanding. "It's a bittersweet story. The way he builds his whole life around a dream, only to see it crumble."

"Tragic," Harris added, watching her closely, thoroughly enjoying their back-and-forth commentary. It had his mind buzzing. The surrounding bar hummed with activity, but Harris felt as if they were in their own little world, peeling away the layers and lessons of a story he held close.

The host's voice broke the spell, announcing the countdown to the next question. Gigi glanced at her phone and then back at Harris, a playful glint in her eyes. "Ready for the next round?"

Harris grinned, hoping there were a thousand questions in this game. "Absolutely. Let's win that Crock-Pot."

"Which Italian dish is traditionally made with arborio rice, broth, and saffron?" the host asked over the speakers. Gigi replied in less than a second.

"Risotto alla Milanese." She spoke with confidence, her fingers flying to select the answer. Her phone screen went green, confirming she was correct.

Harris raised an eyebrow, impressed. "Wow. You really know your Italian food. Though I shouldn't be surprised after the unbelievable soup you whipped up out of her purse."

"It was a tote bag." Gigi chuckled, a faint blush coloring her cheeks. "Nonna taught me to be resourceful."

"You kept us fed through the biggest snowstorm of the season. Very well fed. Now I dream of Italian Penicillin." And of evenings in the kitchen with Gigi.

"I love to cook. It's my way of showing love and making people happy." Their gazes locked and Gigi's cheeks reddened. Had she just insinuated love for him? Harris mulled it over, wondering if it was a slip of the tongue, or if there'd been some truth to it. Not that he thought she loved him, but he hoped she cared. Because he cared for her. Maybe more than he wanted to admit.

"You're an amazing cook," he said, breaking the awkward silence.

"Thank you." Gigi smiled bashfully. "I probably shouldn't tell this to my boss, but if I could make a living out of cooking, I'd do it in a heartbeat." She picked up her mug, cupping it with both hands and holding it just below her mouth.

"What would you do?" Harris urged, leaning an inch closer, genuinely intrigued. "Start a restaurant? Sell at farmer's markets?"

Gigi took a sip of her hot toddy, her eyes sparkling. "I've thought about starting a food delivery service. Imagine sending a package of homemade Italian goodness to a loved one when they were sick or just because—like sending flowers, but tastier."

Harris grinned. "I love that idea."

She thrummed her fingers on her mug. "I'd cook up all kinds of goodies. Comfort foods. Desserts. Chicken parmigiana, risotto, lasagna. Cannoli and panna cotta. And, of course, Italian Penicillin."

"Of course. You can't forget the Penicillin. It's the cure-all and should be the staple in your offering." His stomach growled at the thought. "Why don't you do it? You could combine your love of cooking with your marketing skills. You'd be unstoppable."

Gigi chuckled, a hint of shyness in her laugh. "Thanks. It's just a dream for now."

"Why does it have to be a dream?" His gaze locked on hers. "You've got the skills, Gigi. I've seen your marketing work. It's top-notch. And your passion for cooking is clear. You could definitely make it happen."

Gigi's eyes softened, and she reached out, her fingers brushing against his again, sending a warm shiver down his spine. "You really think so?"

"Absolutely. I'd be your first customer," Harris said sincerely. The desire to reach out and take her hand was overwhelming, but he pushed it down. Normally, he was confident and comfortable making the first move, but this was different. This was Gigi. Their relationship carried the weight of professional boundaries—he was her boss, and the last thing he wanted was for her to feel pressured into anything romantic. Not to mention, he didn't want that for himself either. He wanted something true and real with her.

Harris's heart bounded with Gigi near. He longed to bridge the distance between them, to kiss her, to be with her. But Harris needed Gigi to make the first move. He needed to be absolutely certain she wanted him to touch her, to kiss her, to explore the possibility of a deeper, personal connection.

Uncertainty gnawed at him, making him feel vulnerable in a way he hadn't felt in years. For once, he couldn't take charge. He had to wait for her, and the waiting was torture.

Thankfully, the server arrived with their nachos, distracting Harris from his agony and giving him a moment to recoup his thoughts. She slid a massive platter onto the table. There was a pool of creamy nacho cheese covering a mountain of tortilla chips, grilled chicken, black olives, and jalapenos. On the side, there were bowls of sour cream, salsa, and guacamole.

Harris leaned back, taking in the colossal size of the dish. A laugh escaped his lips. "Wow," he exclaimed, a grin spreading across his face. "You weren't kidding about the nachos being loaded."

Gigi rubbed her hands together like she couldn't wait to dig in.

"Enjoy," the server said, setting down a stack of napkins that Harris was sure they'd need.

"Thank you," Gigi replied, reaching for a chip. She lifted it, watching the cheese drip before sliding it into her mouth. "Oh my God," she mumbled, her eyes fluttering. "These are the best."

Harris joined her and immediately understood her elation. "I'm definitely getting heartburn tonight, but I don't even care."

Gigi laughed, and they spread the sour cream, guacamole, and salsa over their mountain of nachos.

"These are incredible," Harris said, savoring the indulgent flavors right along with the company.

They'd made a small dent in the nachos when Gigi's phone lit up again, announcing the next trivia question would be live soon.

She licked cheese off her thumb, tidied her mouth with a napkin, and picked up her phone.

Harris took a swig of water and leaned close to Gigi, watching the countdown on her phone. When the question appeared, they both groaned.

Who holds the record for the most career passing touchdowns in the NFL?

"You have a guess?" Gigi asked Harris. "I have no idea."

Harris read through the multiple-choice answers, but before he could even guess, some guy in the bar shouted, "Tom Brady! Duh!"

Gigi's head snapped up like someone had called her name. Her expression tightened, and Harris followed her gaze, spotting a guy near the bar. His voice was obnoxiously loud as he went on about how Tom Brady was the greatest of all time, that no one could ever beat his record. Someone at another table shushed him. Gigi's excitement and warmth immediately disappeared, replaced by a look of rigid dread.

"Gigi, you okay?" he asked, protective instincts flaring up.

She swallowed, continuing to stare at the football guy. "Not really. That's my ex-boyfriend."

"Your ex?" She didn't confirm right away, and Harris's stomach dropped. Did she still have a thing for him?

"Yeah, that's Keith," she murmured, her voice tight, before shaking her head and breaking her stare. "He dumped me on Valentine's Day. Took me to my favorite restaurant, knowing he was going to break my heart. Then he left me. Alone. With the bill. I haven't been back to that restaurant since. And they have a to-die-for manicotti."

"He did what?" A surge of hot anger hit Harris in the gut, not understanding how anyone could do that, but especially to Gigi. "What a jerk." He had worse names in mind, but kept his mouth clean. "Do you want me to take care of him for you?"

His question caught Gigi's attention. Her sweet chocolate eyes slid to his. "Like what? Take him out back and give him a knuckle sandwich?"

"I would, if you wanted me to."

She smirked, but shook her head. "He's not worth it."

Harris glanced at Keith. He was sporting a popped collar like it was 1999 and he lived in a frat house. "I feel like he's worth it."

Just then, Keith turned from the bar, cocktail in hand, and his gaze landed on Gigi. Surprise washed over him before he turned to grab a young blonde woman. Draping his arm around the woman's shoulders, he pulled her with him. And they walked straight toward Gigi and Harris.

Gigi swore a few times before they got to the table.

"Gigi! Long time, no see!" Keith's voice dripped with arrogance, and he teetered a bit. It was probably not his first cocktail of the night. The woman under his arm was dressed in an oddly short dress, considering it was freezing outside. She looked confused, but was smiling, crushed against his chest.

"Hey, Keith." Gigi acknowledged him curtly, her tone devoid of the warmth she'd shown Harris all night.

"This is my fiancée, Apple," Keith said, giving the blonde woman a hefty squeeze.

"Apple?" Gigi asked. Harris also wondered if he'd heard the name correctly.

"Yeah, like the fruit," Apple bubbled. "Keith calls me his little Appletini. And he's my Keithy-poo." She laughed, staring adoringly up at Keith. Harris cringed.

"We're celebrating our engagement." Keith reached down and tugged Apple's arm up, practically shoving an enormous ring in Gigi's face.

"Oh." Gigi's head jerked back, like she'd been pushed. "Congratulations."

"Thanks. I can't wait to marry this one." Keith lost his balance and stepped to the side. He took Apple with him. "And you know how opposed to marriage I've always been. Right, Gigi?"

Gigi's jaw tightened. The flash of anger and hurt in her eyes was unmistakable. At least to Harris. Keith, on the other hand, seemed oblivious. Or he was enjoying her pain. Harris sat up straight, disgusted at either option.

"I can't believe I finally found someone to tie me down," Keith continued, giving Apple a shake like she was a rag doll. "My little Appletini."

Keith's blatant insensitivity made Harris's stomach roll, but he tamped down the urge to tell the guy to kick rocks. Instead, he leaned closer to Gigi. He placed a reassuring hand on her arm, wanting her to know he was here for support.

"Congratulations," Harris said evenly, keeping his tone civil. "We were just in the middle of trivia," he added, cuing Keith and Apple to go about their way.

Keith's eyes flicked to Harris, sizing him up. "Who's this?" A smug smile played on his lips. Harris's fingers itched to whack it off.

But before Harris could answer, Gigi replied with, "This is my boyfriend."

Harris's heart stopped. It took a second for Gigi's words to register, but when he caught her gaze, it was all the confirmation he needed. Through a silent stare, Gigi pleaded for him to play along. A surge of adrenaline coursed through his veins, and he turned his head, meeting Keith's entitled gaze head-on.

"That's right," Harris chimed in with a wide smile. "I'm Gigi's boyfriend, Harris."

Chapter Fifteen

Gigi thought she'd be fine when Keith walked over. After all, getting him out of her life was a blessing—one she could only see in hindsight. But having him rub his engagement in her face, with no regard to her feelings, brought her back to that restaurant on Valentine's Day, when she'd been abandoned and humiliated. An old wound ripped open, but it wasn't because she wanted anything to do with Keith. His disregard had exposed her deep-seated fear of not being chosen, of not being good enough. She'd wanted to be with Keith, no matter how insane that sounded to her now. But he'd obviously been holding out for someone prettier, skinnier, and at least ten years younger than her.

Hurt washed through her. She had a strong urge to tell Keith off, but the words got stuck in her throat. And when Harris put his hand on her arm, she turned to him, pausing when she found his gaze a deeper green than she was used to. The strong lines of his face had gone sharp. His broad shoulders had somehow widened. He looked intense, menacing, like he might really drag Keith out in the back alley.

Her heart quivered. Was he concerned? Protective? Of her? Gigi knew what a catch Harris was—kind, intelligent, and incredibly handsome. He was a real man. Someone that would stand up for her, even if it was just as friends.

A crazy impulse shot through her, and it went straight to her mouth.

"This is my boyfriend," Gigi announced, wanting Keith and his fruity fiancée to know she was worthy of someone who truly cared for her, someone like Harris. Though as soon as the lie escaped her, fear gripped her chest, especially as Harris's eyes widened. She hadn't thought through the repercussions of her statement. The only person she truly cared about in this scenario was Harris, and she'd just put him in an incredibly uncomfortable situation.

But just as quickly as his eyes had widened, the surprise swept from Harris's face.

"That's right," he said, giving her a squeeze of support with his hand. "I'm Gigi's boyfriend, Harris." Then he turned to Keith, smiling sharply, like a shark about to rip into a seal. He zoned in on Keith and rose from his chair, his full frame soon a head higher than her ex's, and with the two of them face-to-face, Gigi was acutely aware of their differences. Keith wasn't in the same league as Harris. Not even close. He couldn't touch Harris's class, intelligence, or wit with a ten-foot pole.

"And who are you?" Harris asked, extending his hand to shake Keith's.

"Uh-uh . . . Keith. Keith McCleod." He stuttered while enduring Harris's stiff handshake, which hauled him forward a step. Keith took his hand back, wiggling his fingers like they'd lost circulation.

"I got that much. I meant, who are you to Gigi?" Harris asked, and Gigi stifled a laugh.

"We, uh. Gigi and I dated."

Harris made a dismissive noise, deep in his throat. "That's funny. She's never mentioned you."

"You guys just started dating then?" Keith's mouth went to a straight line, and Gigi chuckled, wondering if he came out of the womb, thinking the world revolved around him.

"We started dating back in February. The day after Valentine's Day." Harris licked his bottom lip, like he enjoyed playing with Keith. "But it feels like we've been together forever. Right, baby?"

Gigi smiled, thoroughly enjoying the show and how it sounded when Harris called her "baby." "Feels like it's been forever," she replied, leaning forward to rest an elbow on the table. She held Harris's gaze, feeling her confidence creeping back in.

"Right after Valentine's Day?" Keith's voice went up an octave. "How . . . how'd you guys meet?"

Harris stared intently at Gigi, looking straight into her soul, and she wondered if he'd ever been an actor. Because he was playing this up. He should win an Oscar for this performance. Gigi was going to buy him a trophy. She barely remembered what Keith had asked until Harris spun a story.

"At a bookstore," Harris said, smirking playfully at Gigi. "We both reached for a book at the same time. Our hands touched, and Gigi spilled her coffee on me. I was smitten. I'd never been so happy to have hot coffee soaking my shirt and burning my chest."

Gigi's grin skated into a full smile. She laughed, wanting to play along. "The book was a special edition of *The Great Gatsby*," she added, keeping her voice steady. "The publisher had just released it that day, and we were both desperate to find a copy."

"Instead, we found each other."

"It was fate."

A spark—a real one—shot between them. The current zipped up and down her spine, and Gigi swallowed. She'd never been this drawn to anyone in her life, and for a second, she let herself hang out in that space. After all, she was currently pretending to be Harris's girlfriend.

"I'm beyond lucky that fate intervened, sending me to a bookstore I'd never been to before, just so I could meet this beautiful woman," Harris added. "We started talking about the book, and before we knew it, an entire evening had passed. We've been inseparable since."

"Seriously?" Apple leaned in, her eyes wide with curiosity. "That is so romantic!"

Harris grinned, his gaze never leaving Gigi's. "It was. It is. Gigi's incredible. I could never let her slip away. Only an idiot would."

Keith cleared his throat, looking annoyed. "Well, that's . . . just wonderful."

Harris's lips tilted into a crooked smile. Gigi returned it, warmth filling her like the first bite of freshly baked bread. Strangely enough, she hoped Keith and Apple would stick around so she could continue this charade with Harris. She didn't want him to stop looking at her like he was.

Just then, the host announced a break in the trivia game. Lively music started playing over the bar's speakers, and the first few chords were instantly recognizable. A group of girls cheered at a table near the bar.

"Do you hear that?" Harris asked Gigi, his gaze tipping upward like musical notes played above his head. "They're playing our song."

Keith's face scrunched in confusion. His arm dropped from Apple's shoulders. "Your song is Shania Twain's 'I Feel Like a Woman'?"

Gigi couldn't help but to laugh. It bubbled up from her belly.

"It's an inside joke. You'd never get it." Harris shrugged at Keith before reaching for Gigi. "Dance with me?"

Gigi stood from her chair, placing her hand in Harris's, a sense of peace and gratitude swirling in her chest. "I'd love to."

Locking her fingers with his, Gigi followed Harris, leaving Keith and Apple behind. He guided her to an open space between a few tables and the bar. With a firm but tender touch, he drew her close. One hand clasped hers, the other settled on her waist, and he swayed them into a slow rhythm that had nothing to do with the upbeat song.

"That should shut him up." His face was all hard lines and his gaze flicked past her, toward Keith. Though she didn't care about Keith anymore. Harris was with her, holding her, making her feel special. This was where she wanted to be, and who she wanted to focus on.

"Thank you for doing that. I shouldn't have put you on the spot like that."

His gaze shifted back to hers. "Don't apologize. I wanted to take that guy into the back alley and give him a knuckle sandwich, remember? You saved me from jail." With a blink, his hard stare went soft, making her knees weak as Jell-O.

"You make an amazing fake boyfriend," she said, trying to tamp the longing in her voice. Could Harris tell she was imagining what it would be like to be together, for real?

He pressed his lips together, keeping his thoughts to himself. His fingers curled on her waist, pulling her closer, and Gigi's heart bounded as she eased into his embrace. Her body conformed to his. Her heart thumped against his solid chest, keeping time with the erratic drums and electric guitars popping over the speakers.

There's something real here, right? She couldn't be that crazy. Harris couldn't be that good of an actor. Whatever it was, Gigi lost herself in it. She lost herself in Harris. She set her cheek on his chest, and they swayed to the music. Before she knew it, Shania sung the last chorus, leaving Gigi wishing for an encore. "I Feel Like a Woman" had taken on a whole new meaning for her.

Gigi picked up her head, looking at Harris. "I liked that even better than trivia," she whispered as the music faded.

"I did too," he replied, holding her even though the song was done. "And I really enjoyed our trivia game."

Butterflies the size of pigeons swarmed her belly. Just then, a slow song started, reigniting Gigi's hope to stay in Harris's embrace.

Harris shifted, his cheek dipping close to hers as he asked, "Stay with me for another dance?" His breath tickled her neck, sending a shiver down her spine. Anticipation snatched at her chest.

"Okay," she said, surprised to hear a tremor in her answer, but Harris didn't let her focus on the waver. He guided both her hands to the back of his neck before looping his arms around her middle. Then he took hold of her, using his height to draw her in, bending her back ever so slightly, bringing their faces inches apart.

"Gigi," he started, his voice low and intimate, touching Gigi in all the right spots. "You deserve to be treated like a queen, always. I hope you know that."

She went speechless. Shortly after, they'd stopped swaying, fully wrapped up in each other, their gazes tied together with an invisible rope. This close, Gigi could count every emerald fleck and streak of blue in Harris's soulful eyes. They captured her and drew her in like a powerful river current.

His arms tightened, pulling her impossibly closer. Heat radiated from his body. Or was that hers? Their hearts beat in sync—against each other—and her gaze flicked to his lips. Would he kiss her? Because that was all she was thinking about.

Leaning in, Harris gave Gigi's heart a start. But instead of meeting her lips, he shifted course, grazing her neck with his soft mouth as he whispered, "I won't kiss you like this."

His warm breath. The brush of his lips. His velvet voice.

Goosebumps rushed over her, all the way to her toes. She was putty in his hands. Her body arched back, trusting entirely in Harris to keep her from falling.

"How would you kiss me?" she countered, breathless.

Harris took entirely too long to reply. "If I kiss you, it needs to be special, and at the right time. Most importantly, it can't be fake. I want to kiss you, Gigi. That's real. But I need to be one hundred percent certain it's what you want too."

For a moment, she was lost in the shock wave of his whispers, knowing that he wanted to kiss her too. Then, with a surge of courage, Gigi said, "I'm one hundred percent certain, Harris. Take me somewhere to kiss me."

Chapter Sixteen

Harris paid the bill and stuffed his wallet into his coat pocket. Gigi took his hand, and as they weaved through the crowd at the bar, Harris considered following Gigi anywhere. He'd wanted to kiss her as they danced—so badly, he'd nearly combusted—but he wasn't about to have their first kiss be a façade. He didn't want her ex watching. Harris wanted Gigi to himself. He wanted their kiss to snowball into something real. Something far beyond a moment.

Holding tight to Gigi's hand, he couldn't believe he'd gotten here, and so quickly. Falling for someone wasn't on his agenda. It wasn't why he came to Chicago, and it certainly didn't make the challenges with his father any easier.

But Gigi wasn't just someone.

She'd hooked him with her kind heart, quick wit, and fierce determination. He'd thought of her every spare second. He wanted to be by her side at all hours.

None of that was normal—not for him. Harris didn't trip over himself on the way to any woman. In fact, he wasn't sure he even believed in love. But how he felt around Gigi was something he'd never experienced. And he wanted more.

Bursting out the door, they shuffled into the cold. It was late, but city lights illuminated the street. Traffic bustled by, headlights shining. Streetlamps glowed, spotlighting the falling snow. Harris dug in his pocket for his phone, ready to call for the valet. "I'll have my car brought around. A friend of mine owns The Signature Room at the Ninety-Fifth. Amazing views of the city and the chef makes a million different flavors of cheesecake. I'll call him and reserve the lounge—"

Gigi clasped his hand, stopping him mid-sentence. "I don't care where we go, Harris," she said, her voice soft but firm. "I only care that I'm with you. Kiss me here. This is perfect."

Harris stared at her, amazed that she was solely focused on him, not on what he could give her or where he could take her. Snowflakes swirled around them, salting her mahogany hair. The neon bar sign glowed across her face, and her eyes shone with sincerity. Realizing this moment, right here in front of the bar, was more perfect than any grand gesture he could've planned, Harris closed the short distance to Gigi. He cupped her face, sweeping his thumbs across her blushed cheeks.

"I'm going to kiss you now," he whispered. When Gigi responded by biting her bottom lip, barely disguising a smile, Harris leaned in, heart pounding.

He pressed his lips to hers, and everything around the two of them dissolved. The cold wind. The falling snow. The buzz of traffic. It was all replaced by their intense connection. Harris absorbed Gigi's sweet scent, savored every touch. His fingers laced into her hair, and her arms wrapped around his neck. Unspoken words filled every movement, containing all the emotions he'd been holding back.

When he thought his heart might explode, Harris pulled back. He rested his forehead against hers. "You have no idea how long I've wanted to do that," he murmured, his breath mingling with hers.

Gigi's eyes fluttered open, and she smiled. "Probably as long as I've wanted you to."

He chuckled, relief washing over him. "Glad we're both on the same page."

Her eyes sparkled. "Same book. Same page."

Gigi rose onto her tiptoes, pulling him into another kiss, and Harris couldn't help himself. He lifted her into his arms, desire igniting as she wrapped her legs around his waist. Tightening his hold, he deepened the kiss, his stomach spinning as she melted into him.

In that moment, he knew their connection was real. And now that Harris had a taste, he couldn't back away. This was the start of something special, and Harris wanted to explore whatever came next, even though it terrified him.

Harris stood in Dean's corner office, admiring the panoramic view of the Chicago skyline, which was on full display through the large windows. He was in an amazing mood, despite the fact that their father had just blazed in, complained of losing market share, and claimed the company would be bankrupt in a year if Harris and Dean didn't pull their heads out of their rears and do something about it. However, Harris's good mood couldn't be dampened. Memories of his time with Gigi swirled through his mind, keeping his heart light and his spirits high. But he kept those sweet thoughts to himself, for now. He wouldn't risk ruining what was blossoming with Gigi by involving his family—particularly his dad.

Dean glanced up from his desk, raising an eyebrow at Harris. "You look like you've won the lottery. What's going on?"

Harris shrugged, a smirk playing on his lips. "Just had a good weekend, that's all."

Dean scrunched his forehead and set his pen on his desk. "Didn't you work all weekend?"

Harris nodded but didn't comment. Instead, he took a seat in one of the stiff leather chairs that faced the desk. He leaned back, surveying Dean's office. Special memories and people filled the walls. There were pictures of his wife and kids, a framed football jersey from high school, crayon drawings from his youngest. Dean lived a full life outside of this office.

"I've been thinking about Dad's offer," Harris admitted, and Dean's expression shifted to cautious interest.

"How so?"

Harris slid his arm onto the armrest, running his fingers over the leather. "I've been thinking about what it would be like if I stayed."

Dean sat straight up, surprise evident on his face. "Really?! You're considering staying? Permanently? Taking over the company with me?"

Harris grinned at his brother's excitement. "I've enjoyed spending time with you, Cheri, and the kids. It's nice to be close to family again. I've missed you guys."

"We've missed you," Dean said with a wide stare, as if that were obvious. A pang of brotherly love pinched Harris.

"And honestly, I forgot how much I enjoy sales and marketing. It's been refreshing. I've been working behind the scenes with GambleOnLove for so long that I kind of forgot how exhilarating it can be in the trenches."

Dean leaned back in his chair, rocking it. "I didn't expect to hear this. I thought you were all-in with your dating app, that you wanted to get back to New York as soon as possible."

"I did," Harris admitted, rubbing the back of his neck, knowing there were multiple reasons he was now considering staying in Chicago. Gigi was a big part of that. "I'm trying to figure out what to do. I think I could run both companies."

Dean gave him a look like that was a ridiculously bad idea. "You want to run two companies? That's a huge time commitment. Every minute of every day would be taken up with work. Why don't you sell GambleOnLove? Live a little?"

The thought had crossed Harris's mind, but he just couldn't fathom doing it. He sighed and glanced out the window at the gray sky and tall towers. "It was Adam's baby. I feel like I'd be letting him down if I sold it." He could figure out a way to make it work, couldn't he?

Dean's expression softened, knowing what Harris had been through, losing his best friend a few years ago. "I get it, Harris. I do. But Adam would want you to be happy. He wouldn't want you to feel chained to a company for his sake." Dean was quiet for a few moments before he continued. "Listen, I'm just glad to hear you're considering taking over the family business with me. I'm here to support your decision, no matter what—just like you do for me."

Harris turned back to his brother, the tension in his chest cracking. "Thanks."

"We'll figure it out together." Dean nodded, and the weight on Harris's shoulders lessened. Until their dad swooped through the door.

"What are you two doing? Sitting around playing tiddlywinks?" their dad asked, irritation etched on his face, like always.

When was the last time anyone said 'tiddlywinks'? Harris would've laughed, if it were anyone else.

"Hit the phones," their dad continued his rant with a wave of his hand. "Dive into those reports. I want five actionable items to increase market share by tonight." He finished his marching orders and swooped back into the hallway, off to darken someone else's day.

The brothers shared a look. Dean rolled his eyes and scooched his chair over to his computer. "Better get to it," he said.

Harris chewed his bottom lip. "By the way, there is zero percent chance I'll continue working for the family business if dad doesn't retire." He thrummed his fingers against the armrest. "We better put that in the contract."

Chapter Seventeen

"There's a little extra Christmas cheer in this batch," Alice announced, pinching her mouth after a sip of the Mistletoe Margaritas Paige had concocted. "Wowza!" Her head snapped back as she licked the sugar granules from her lips.

"I made them strong," Paige answered in a singsong. She shimmied her shoulders, raising her glass. "It's our Yappy Hour Christmas party. Time to live it up!" She winked. Both Alice and Gigi giggled before they all took sips of the sweetly sour drink garnished with cranberries, a sprig of rosemary, and a sugared glass rim.

It was the last Friday before Christmas, and the girls were celebrating with a slumber party at Alice's apartment. All cozied up in her living room, they were sipping margaritas and sporting Christmas pajamas. A perfectly predictable Christmas romance movie played on the TV, and their tummies were full of Italian Penicillin and home-baked bread. Before work, Gigi had whipped up the soup and it had simmered all day in her new Crock-Pot—the one Harris had surprised her with.

She smiled through another sip, remembering how she'd discovered the package that'd been waiting in her apartment building's mailroom. The card that came with it said, *Even though we got cheated out of winning the trivia game, I still thought you deserved a Crock-Pot. Sincerely Chapped, Harris.*

Her heart warmed at the thoughtful gesture. It was a thousand times better than flowers.

"Okay, time for you guys to open your presents from me." Alice bounced in the recliner. The throw blanket slid from her crossed legs to the floor. Behind her, Mister Tuxedo stretched, rousing from his nap on the back of the chair. Sensing excitement, he sauntered down to the armrest, crawled across Alice's lap, and jumped to the coffee table. There, he collapsed and rubbed his face against a wrapped present.

"You are such a ham." Gigi reached over and scratched him on his white belly and chest. Tux purred, his eyes closing. "I think you'd really like Rudy. You need to convince your momma that you need a little brother." Gigi quirked a brow at Alice, waiting for her reaction.

"If Harris isn't going to keep Rudy, I think *you* need to adopt him. I'll be his godmother." Alice stood to gather the presents.

"Then we can plan playdates for the boys. And Rudy can come for Yappy Hour."

"Wouldn't that be perfect?" Gigi sighed. "Except my apartment doesn't allow pets."

"Do they allow children?" Paige asked.

Gigi nodded. "Of course."

"Then call him your furry son." Paige shrugged. "Besides, I bet he's better behaved than most children."

Gigi laughed, rattling the ice in her drink. "He might be."

"Or, get a note from a therapist and Rudy can be your emotional support cat, just like Mister Tuxedo. Then your landlord can't say no. I can take Tux anywhere. You know how he loves to go for walks in his front pack. Honestly, he always makes me feel better, in any situation." Alice patted Tux before handing Gigi a perfectly wrapped present with sharp corners, neatly tucked ends, and a bow that Martha Stewart would approve of.

"Thank you," Gigi said, referencing both the gift and the suggestion. "I mean, that's not a bad idea. Rudy increases my serotonin levels every time I see him and get cuddles."

"It's a great idea," Alice replied matter-of-factly.

"You should do it." Paige leaned back in her seat after accepting Alice's present. "By the way, why doesn't Harris want to keep him?"

Gigi paused, knowing that Harris clearly loved Rudy. She could see it. His face lit up around the little furball, and he was an amazing cat-dad. "He said he works too much. Wants Rudy to go to a home where he gets all the attention he deserves."

"Well, that's . . . noble," Paige concluded.

"It is," Gigi said. "But he's been doing a great job fostering him. Rudy isn't deprived of attention."

"Maybe he'll change his mind?" Alice sat back down as Tux leaped from the coffee table. He slunk to the base of the pink-frosted artificial tree in the corner of the living room and whacked one of the low-hanging bulbs. "Tuxy, you better not even think about climbing the tree again," she scolded in a tender tone. Tux flattened his ears like that's exactly what he'd been planning to do. Alice smirked at him before turning her attention back to her friends. "Okay, open them!"

Gigi and Paige unraveled the perfect bows.

"It pains me to undo your wrapping. It's such a masterpiece," Gigi said, ripping into the shiny paper. Alice crinkled her nose in delight.

Each year, the three of them exchanged gifts, but the presents had to be handmade, not bought. This year, Gigi spent an entire evening baking specialty desserts. She'd filled two boxes to the brim with cannoli, biscotti, and amaretti cookies, and both Paige and Alice had squealed when they pried open the lids. Paige had given Alice and Gigi advanced copies of her next book, which would release after the New Year. Each was signed with personal messages, and she'd also framed pictures of the three of them from their girls' trip to Mexico earlier that year. Paige cheated a little by not making the frames herself, but Alice and Gigi gave her a pass. That was as close to handmade as Paige got.

Alice's gifts were the last to open. Opening the box and tugging out white tissue paper, Gigi discovered Alice's beautiful knitting.

"Oh, wow! These are adorable!" Gigi exclaimed, holding up two pairs of fuzzy socks for Paige to see. One pair was striped red and green with tiny pom-poms around the cuffs. The other was covered in kittens. "Look at these details!" Gigi put on the striped socks and wiggled her toes, delighting in the softness and shaking pom-poms. "I'm going to wear these every day!"

"I'm so glad you like them." Alice beamed, squeezing her hands together. "There's one more thing in there."

Gigi dug around in the box to pull out a hand-knit cat toy in the shape of Santa, complete with gold bells. "For Rudy?" Gigi gaped.

"For Rudy," Alice confirmed.

Gigi jumped up and hugged Alice. "Thank you. I love them. You are so thoughtful," she whispered.

"You are very welcome." Alice hugged her back. "Now it's your turn, Paige."

Paige's eyes widened as she opened her present to find a lilac knitted beanie, as well as a matching set of fingerless gloves. "Alice, these are incredible!" She pulled the beanie over her black hair and slid on the gloves, wiggling her exposed fingertips. "These are perfect for staying cozy and still being able to type and write. How did you find the time to make all of this?"

Alice blushed, shrugging modestly. "I love knitting, and I always make time for my favorite people."

The three friends hugged and clinked their margarita glasses together, toasting to their friendship and a very Merry Christmas.

Smiling at her friends, a wave of gratitude washed over Gigi. She was beyond blessed to have two best friends who felt like sisters, and she'd never take that for granted. Her heart was full as they chatted the evening away, talking and laughing about everything under the sun.

As they were belly laughing through Paige's rendition of her last blind date, courtesy of GambleOnLove, Gigi's phone buzzed on the coffee table. She glanced at the screen, her heart skipping a beat. "It's Harris," she said, surprised.

Paige and Alice exchanged amused glances.

"Ooooh, Harris!" Alice teased, waggling her eyebrows. "What's he calling for so late? Wanting to meet you under the mistletoe?"

"Pick up and put him on speaker." Paige leaned forward with interest. "I'm going to give him an earful about his app matching me up with the vegan guy from the suburbs who spends every waking minute tending to his indoor hydroponic garden." She raised a brow, ready to give him a piece of her mind.

Gigi smirked, but her cheeks flushed as she picked up the phone, pressing it to her ear. "Hello? Harris?" He knew she was with Paige and Alice tonight, so she wasn't sure why he'd be calling. Maybe he just wanted to wish her a good night.

But when Harris spoke, that sweet thought vanished from her mind.

"Gigi, I'm so sorry to call you this late." His tone was tight and panicked, sending a chill through Gigi. "Rudy is missing, and I don't know what to do."

Chapter Eighteen

Harris paced the sidewalk outside his brownstone, his breath puffs of steam in the frigid night air. He'd been searching for Rudy for what felt like an eternity, but it'd only been half an hour, though a lot could happen to a tiny kitten in a short window. It wasn't supposed to get above ten degrees tonight and the wind was picking up, dusting spirals of snow over passing cars. Harris's heart raced with worry, thinking of poor, lost Rudy, shaking in the cold or wandering into traffic. His stomach turning with dread, Harris scanned the street again, his eyes darting to every shadow and flickering light, but there was no sign of the little orange kitten.

Harris checked his phone, thinking he might have missed a call or text from one of the neighbors he'd already talked to, but there were no messages. He'd also contacted Animal Control but could only leave a voicemail. They were closed for the evening, so he wouldn't hear until tomorrow if they'd taken Rudy in. Harris's heart sank, and he started down the sidewalk again, calling for Rudy as he double-checked the neighbor's entrance and around their stairwell.

Just then, a taxi pulled up to the curb, and the doors swung open. Gigi and her friends jumped out, bundled in coats, hats, and scarves.

"How long do you think he's been outside?" Gigi ran to him, her face etched with worry, her friends not far behind her. All three of them turned on flashlights, which beamed into the night.

"Probably a couple of hours." Harris ran a hand over his mouth and chin, trying to control the horrid thoughts racing through his head. "I was working late at the office and asked my property manager to stop over and feed Rudy. He must've slipped out the front door when he left. I've been searching everywhere, but I can't find him. It's so cold out here, and I'm worried sick."

Gigi nodded and swallowed, her face mirroring his dread. She turned to her friends. "Alice, Paige, this is Harris." They acknowledged each other with terse nods, and Harris wished he wasn't meeting Gigi's best friends like this, in a horrible situation that he'd caused.

Paige looped her scarf around her neck as she scanned the darkened street. "Let's split up and cover more ground."

Harris agreed, grateful for their support. "I've checked the alley and the neighboring yards, but he could be anywhere. Someone could've picked him up."

Gigi placed a hand on his arm, bringing his attention to her. "Don't worry, we'll find him." But the confidence in her statement deepened his anxiety. Harris desperately wanted Rudy safe, and if he couldn't make that happen, he was going to break Gigi's heart right along with his own.

"Why don't you and Alice start on the other side of the street," Gigi suggested to Paige. "I'll stick with Harris closer to his house."

The four of them fanned out, calling Rudy's name, and peering into every nook and cranny. A lump rose in Harris's throat as he called out again and again, his voice echoing into the night. Gigi's voice mimicked his, and there was a small measure of comfort knowing she was there with him.

"Rudy! Rudy!" they called, their voices a chorus of desperate hope.

Minutes ticked by, each one stretching longer than the last. They shuffled through snow, knocked on doors, peered into doorways and under parked cars. Harris's fingers and toes had gone numb from the cold, but he didn't care. He had to find Rudy. The thought of any pain coming to the sweet kitten was unbearable. When a stiff gust of wind made him shiver, Harris considered telling Gigi, Paige, and Alice to take a break and warm up in his house while he continued searching, but a screechy meow stopped Harris in his tracks.

"Rudy?" he called, but Gigi was already running toward the noise, her flashlight scanning the front of a brownstone only a few houses down from his.

"Oh, my God, he's here!" Gigi called, falling to her knees in the snow. Harris was at her side in the blink of an eye, and they both peered down into a basement window well. Gigi's flashlight illuminated the deep, snowy window well, identifying a shivering orange kitten tucked up next to the brick.

Rudy screeched, looking up at them with pitiful eyes, and Harris dropped to his stomach. He reached into the well, and as soon as he felt fur, Harris grasped him and scooped him out. His heart leapt into his throat. "Rudy?" Harris scanned the shaking kitten as he and Gigi sat stunned in a mound of snow.

"Is he okay?" Gigi breathed, her voice cracking as she leaned close. Rudy mewed again, like he couldn't believe they'd found him. His orange coat was crusted in snow.

"I think so." Other than looking horribly cold, Rudy didn't seem to be hurt. Harris unzipped his jacket, tucking the kitten gently inside, against his chest. His little paws were like ice cubes. "Let's get him inside."

Gigi nodded, and they stood from the snow. Heading back toward Harris's house, Gigi called out for Alice and Paige. They called back and quickly cut across the road.

"You found him?" Alice yelled, scooting between two parked cars just a step behind Paige.

"He was in a window well," Gigi said, frowning in sympathy.

"Oh, poor thing!" Paige peered into Harris's jacket as the kitten let out a pitiful meow.

Harris cradled his little body tightly against his chest, wanting Rudy to know he was safe.

Leading the group into his house, Harris welcomed the warmth, but the silence that surrounded them was still thick with worry. He went straight to the fireplace, turning it on as Gigi grabbed a blanket from the couch. She approached Harris, gently removing Rudy from his coat and wrapping him in the blanket. Sitting down on the floor next to the glowing fireplace, Gigi cradled Rudy close. Her expression was a mix of relief and concern as she rubbed the kitten, getting his circulation going and drying him.

"I'm going to get him some food," Harris said and headed for the kitchen. When he returned with a bowl of wet paté, he paused, taking in the scene. All three women were on the ground in a circle around Rudy. Their coats, scarves, and hats were discarded in piles behind them. Harris realized they were all wearing flannel Christmas pajamas, and the thought of how the wind and cold must have bitten through the material struck him. No one had complained about being cold.

Before them, Rudy relaxed on the blanket. He was being petted and coddled as the fire warmed him. The sight gave Harris an inkling of relief.

He neared and joined the circle, kneeling to set down the bowl of food. Rudy blinked up at Harris. A soft mew escaped his mouth and Harris reached out to stroke his head. The kitten purred, and Harris's heart clenched.

"You need to eat." Harris pushed the bowl close to Rudy. The kitten sniffed, easing the ache in Harris's chest when he took a bite.

After some food, Rudy began to perk up, but Harris still called an emergency vet. While waiting for the house call and checkup, he brewed a pot of tea and cooked a frozen pizza for Gigi, Alice, and Paige. When the vet arrived, he confirmed Rudy was fine, despite Harris's fears of hypothermia and frostbite.

"Just keep doing what you're doing," the vet consoled Harris as he left. "You're doing a great job and Rudy is a champ."

"Thanks, doc," Harris said, showing him out. As he did, Paige and Alice gathered their coats.

"Our Uber is almost here," Paige announced. "You coming or staying?" She looked at Gigi for an answer.

"I think I'll stay," Gigi said, but glanced at Harris for confirmation. "If that's okay with you?"

"I'd like that," he replied, before thanking them all for rushing over. "I wish we'd met on better terms, but I don't know what I would have done without your help. Thank you."

"We're just glad Rudy's okay," Paige said, covering a yawn.

Alice looked between Harris and Gigi, adding, "If you need anything else, don't hesitate to call."

Gigi saw them out before gathering the sleepy kitten from the couch. She cuddled Rudy to her chest and looked at Harris. "Did you eat anything? You took care of everyone else, but I haven't seen you eat anything."

Harris shook his head. "I don't have an appetite." He'd been starving when he got home until he realized Rudy wasn't in the house.

"Come on," Gigi urged gently. "Let's at least get comfortable. Turn on a show or something?"

He nodded, and they moved to the back of the house, settling in the living room. Gigi tucked Rudy in a blanket on the couch, wrapping him snugly. Then she plugged in the Christmas lights and turned on the television, putting the volume at a low hum. As she did, Harris cleaned up the kitchen. He packed the leftover pizza into a Ziploc and set it in the fridge.

Gigi watched before joining him in the kitchen. "You need to quit beating yourself up over this."

He sighed, running a hand through his hair. "I should've been home. If I hadn't stayed late at work, this never would've happened."

Gigi's eyes softened. She stepped close, putting a hand on his arm, but her touch felt heavy, a stark reminder of how he'd failed. "Harris, you can't blame yourself. Accidents happen. The important thing is that Rudy's safe now."

"But what if he wasn't?" Harris stilled, looking down and closing his eyes for a moment, thinking of Adam. The night his best friend died, Harris was supposed to meet him for dinner. "I put him in danger because I wasn't here when I should have been. This is exactly why he needs a better home."

Gigi tilted her head, looking confused. "You love him. You wouldn't be so upset if you didn't. Rudy has a great home with you." Her lips parted like she didn't believe what he was saying. "You can't live your life in fear of what might happen, Harris. Caring comes with risks, but it also comes with joy and love. Rudy is lucky to have you. So am I."

Harris looked at her, a strange mix of gratitude and doubt hitting him in the chest. The fear of loving and losing was overwhelming. "I just . . . I don't know if I'm cut out for this."

Gigi scanned his face, flicking to his gaze. She blinked, suddenly looking lost. "Harris, are we still talking about Rudy?"

Her grip loosened, reminding him of the risk that came with letting someone in. Fear cascaded down around him, filling the room like a sinking boat. He didn't know how to plug the hole.

In his silence, Gigi's puzzled expression turned to hurt. She dropped her hand. "Maybe I should go." Her disappointment cut through him like a knife, and when she stepped back, Harris realized the gravity of his mistake. He just wasn't sure how to make it better.

"Please stay." He reached out, grasping hold of her fingertips. Gigi paused, but Harris struggled to find the words to express what was running through his mind, what he was truly scared of. It wasn't loving her—it was the idea of losing her that frightened him.

Chapter Ninteen

A sharp sting seized Gigi's throat. Had she been a complete fool? Was Harris pushing her away? He was distant and wrapped up in his own thoughts—completely different from the engaging, affectionate man he'd been with her just the other night. What had changed in a few short days?

"Maybe I should go," she determined, feeling her own defenses rise. Was she wrong to think there was something special between them? Maybe Harris didn't want the same things she did. Maybe he didn't want her. Gigi's chest clenched at the thought of his rejection. She'd finally opened her heart, and it was about to be swatted to the ground.

Dropping her hand, she stepped back, feeling like she couldn't reach him, wherever his mind was.

"Please stay," Harris said, and she stilled when he took her hand.

Harris curled his fingers around hers, and they stood there, locked together with a simple grasp, surrounded by a slurry of emotions. In that moment, the raw vulnerability in his stare struck her. It gave her pause, even though she had a strong urge to back away. She had to know what he was thinking before more walls flew up.

Taking a deep breath, Gigi steadied her own fears in an attempt to understand him. "Harris, what's going on? What's wrong?"

His jaw clenched, and he swallowed. His Adam's apple bobbed up and down, and Gigi braced herself for what he was about to say.

"I haven't been honest with you." He tightened his grip on her hand, like he knew she was about to pull away.

Her stomach bottomed out, heavy with uncertainty. "You haven't been honest? You've been lying to me?"

"No. I didn't lie." He shook his head. "I just didn't expect to fall for you, and that brings a whole different perspective to why I'm here. There's a lot I didn't tell you."

Her heart fluttered at the first part of his confession, but the sting of his distance was still fresh in her head, so she tried her best to ignore it.

"What do you mean?" she asked, staring at him, looking for the truth somewhere amidst what he was telling her. She steeled herself, her grandma's words loud in her head. *Don't waste your precious time with anyone that doesn't show you love.* Gigi needed to know what was going through his head, and how he truly felt about her. She didn't want to guess anymore. "Harris, I need you to be very clear with me right now, because I'm really confused."

Harris took both of her hands, clasped them together, and encircled them with his. He stared straight into her soul. "I didn't come back to the family business by choice, and I never intended to stay."

Gigi's heart pounded. And not in a good way. "What do you mean?"

"My father didn't give me a choice. Either I came back to Ryan & Ryan, or he'd sell the company, specifically to our largest competitor."

She exhaled, surprise slipping past her lips. "He did? I had no idea. Dean was okay with that?" The picture Harris painted frightened her. Would she even have a job if the company was acquired?

"No, Dean wasn't okay with it. That's why I came back, to help him change our dad's mind. I was going to stay through the holidays and work, appeasing my dad while I figured out how to convince him to sell the company to my brother. I came back for Dean. He's always wanted to take over. He's the one with the passion for the business. Not me."

"But, I—" Gigi scrunched her brow, her feelings for Harris sidetracked by this revelation. Not to mention, she didn't understand what Harris was saying. She'd witnessed his passion for the business firsthand. Her mind flew back to their conversation in the carriage and how he'd skittered around the subject of moving to New York. "Why'd you leave the company the first time?"

His grip softened. He worried his bottom lip, but she needed answers. Gigi had heard all the gossip and now she wanted it straight from Harris's mouth.

"Back then, I just wanted to go off on my own. I wanted to live my life how I wanted to live it—not under my father's thumb. I was done letting him dictate every part of my life, which he enjoys doing. I needed to make my own money and my own way. Leaving the company felt like my only option. But it also put me in a horrible place with my family, and I wish I hadn't made that decision so hastily."

"Your dad wasn't happy that you left," she concluded, the dark of the kitchen casting shadows across his face.

"My father never supported my choice to start my own business," Harris began, his voice low, his head tipped down toward her. "When I told him about starting the dating app with Adam, he was furious. Said I was an idiot—amongst many other choice words. To him, it was a slap in the face, to leave the business he'd built." He pressed his lips together, forming a flat line. "Dad and I didn't talk for a very long time. Even now, our relationship is rocky. Dean didn't understand either. It even took us a few years to see eye to eye again. That hurt the most, because Dean and I had always been close."

A pang of sympathy hit her chest, and she appreciated hearing Harris's side of the story. Still, she didn't grasp the complete picture. And she didn't understand how she could fit into it. "So, you came back here to play peacemaker? To help Dean?"

"I'm trying to fix what I messed up."

His words hit Gigi hard. He was here temporarily. Harris wanted to leave.

She swallowed, fighting the reality that *they* were likely temporary too.

"Honestly, I shouldn't be telling you any of this," Harris said, regret coloring his tone.

Gigi's stomach dropped, instantly reminded of the reality of their relationship. Harris was her boss. It was his family she worked for. A knot tightened in her chest, closing around the fact that she shouldn't have gotten her heart involved. Even if Harris didn't continue with the business, could they date if she worked for his father? Was there a scenario where she kept her job and they stayed together? Could she rip up her life and follow him to New York? Did he even want that?

She exhaled, countless scenarios crashing over her, making her wish she could detach her heart from her body. "You don't have to explain yourself to me," she whispered, almost without thinking. She was deflecting, wanting to smother the pain that was about to come.

"I want to," he replied immediately, and she searched his eyes. Harris leaned in, his shoulders squared, his lips parted. "I came back for one purpose. I thought I could get through the holidays, change my father's mind, and go back to New York." His grip on her hands tightened, as if seeking reassurance. "But then I met you."

Hope cut her in the ribs. She wasn't sure what to expect next, but she had to hear it. "And? What does that mean? What do you want from me?" She teetered on the edge of crashing or soaring and braced herself for either.

Harris took a deep breath, his eyes searching hers. "Gigi, you've reignited something in me I thought I'd lost. Passion. Joy. You're like some kind of drug I didn't know I needed. I'm addicted to you."

"What?" Her brow furrowed, not expecting his answer.

"I need more Gigi. I think about you all the time. I'm an addict." He shrugged, as if that were a normal thing to say.

Taken off guard, her lips slowly tilted into a lopsided smile. "I'm your drug?"

"I probably didn't say that right." Harris grinned before he gently tugged her near. She gave in, letting him press her hands over his heart. "What I'm trying to say is that I want to be around you and with you. I care about you, but I also need to be honest and tell you I'm struggling with leaving my life behind in New York."

She paused for a few breaths before nodding. Her heart fluttered like a hummingbird, reacting to the longing in his eyes, but her mind told her she needed more. "What don't you want to leave behind?" She prayed he wouldn't surprise her with "wife" or "girlfriend." This close to him, she'd have a hard time dropkicking him in the head.

Harris ran his thumb over the back of her hand. "GambleOnLove is in New York, but it isn't just a business or income for me. It was my best friend Adam's dream, and he passed two years ago . . ." Harris's voice wavered, and Gigi stilled. She stopped breathing, immediately tightened her grip on his hand.

"Adam died?"

Harris nodded, and Gigi caught the shine in his eyes. It made her heart hurt.

"In a car accident," he added. "I was supposed to meet him for dinner but got wrapped up in a meeting. He grabbed an Uber to cross town and meet me at my house, and it got hit head-on by a drunk driver."

Her hand flew to her mouth, covering a gasp. The silence in the kitchen was deafening. "That's horrible," she muttered past her hand.

Harris blinked, obviously trying to push aside the memory of Adam's passing away. "I promised myself I'd carry on his legacy. It's why I've been so committed to the app. It's not just a company to me. It's a way to keep a part of him alive."

Gigi's eyes welled with tears. "Harris, I didn't know. I'm so sorry."

"I didn't mean to dump all of that on you." His voice was thick with emotion. "But I need you to know where my head is at." He tipped her chin up with a finger. "That was a very long way of me explaining what I'm struggling with ... and telling you, I really like you."

She pressed her lips together, wanting to believe Harris and struggling with her own fear of abandonment. "I really like you too," she replied, strangely following her gut.

"I want to make this work."

Gigi nodded, watching the Christmas lights reflect and sparkle in his eyes, wanting his last statement to be true. They held each other's gazes, and she churned through thoughts, emotions, and worry until Harris closed the gap, gently pressing his lips to hers. He kissed her, slow and tender, then wrapped his arms around her and held her until her doubts eased. They hugged and stayed pressed together long enough that Rudy mewed at them.

Gigi rubbed her fingers in a slow circle on Harris's back. "I think he wants us to join him on the couch."

"I couldn't think of anything better," he replied.

Chapter Twenty

"Hang on a second, Sis," Gigi spoke into the phone, before pulling it from her ear. She'd called her sister, Val, while walking to her favorite coffee shop—the one across the street from her apartment building, where they knew her by name.

Gigi waved at the barista behind the registrar, Nico, who was sporting his signature bowtie and tweed fedora. "The aqua bowtie is killer. Really brings out your eyes."

Nico's face lit up, and he touched his bowtie. "Ms. Gigi, you are the sweetest! What can I get you this beautiful morning?"

"Truck driver coffee," she replied, tipping her head to give him her serious eyes.

"You got it." Nico flipped a paper cup off a stack and scribbled her name across it. "Steaming hot cup of truck driver expresso blend. Room for cream?"

She shook her head, and Nico whistled, raising his brow. "Coming right up." He turned toward the back counter and Gigi pressed the phone to her ear again.

"Okay, I'm back," she said to Val.

"Sissy, *what* is truck driver coffee?"

"It's the kind of coffee you get when you have to drive from here to Florida in one shot."

Val cackled, clearly entertained by Gigi's explanation. "Why do you need that strong of coffee?"

Gigi paused, considering her answer as Nico clicked a top on the steaming cup. "Thanks, Nico." She slid him a bill and told him to put the change in the tip jar. He winked and handed her the cup. "I got sucked into a movie and was up way too late." She padded the truth. In reality, she'd stayed up into the wee hours of the morning, talking with Harris. They watched a movie, but Gigi had been more focused on their conversation and each stolen kiss. They'd talked more about Adam and their families. Conversation spiraled into hopes and dreams. As for the show, she couldn't remember the plotline. She barely remembered the actors.

But Gigi wasn't quite ready to tell her big sis about Harris. Val had taken care of Gigi while their mom worked long hours to keep food on the table, so Val was as much of a mom to Gigi as their mother was. Gigi wanted to be one hundred percent certain of her relationship with Harris before breaking the news to Val. She wouldn't gush to her sister ever again about a man that might not stick around. No matter how crazy she was about him.

"Was it a romance or a murder mystery?" Val asked, knowing Gigi's genres of choice.

"Definitely a romance."

"Any good?"

"*Really* good."

"What's the name of it? Evan and I are picking up pizza tonight and we want to watch a movie. I need a suggestion. With all the snow we've been getting, we've had a lot of movie nights. I think we've watched all the new releases."

"I'll text it to you later." Gigi added a cardboard sleeve to her coffee cup. "But you need to save some movies for me!"

In just a few days, Gigi would fly to Minneapolis—on Christmas Day—where Val would pick her up at the airport. From there, they'd drive four hours north to the charming town of Maple Bay, where Val lived with her fiancé, Evan. Val and Evan had dated in college and, through a crazy twist of fate, had rekindled their romance this past summer. Val had redesigned Evan's house for the fixer-upper reality TV show she hosted.

"I'm going to be there for almost a week, and I definitely want to be curled up next to your fireplace, watching a ton of sappy, funny rom-coms and creepy murder mysteries. We need to make a list." Gigi tapped her chin thoughtfully.

Val giggled. "I think we need a re-watch party. Want to watch all our favorites from childhood?"

Gigi sucked in a breath, loving Val's suggestion. "Yessssssss, let's do it!"

"Issy will love that too," Val added, excitement in her voice as she referred to Evan's teenage daughter. Val and Issy had hit it off from the moment they'd met, and it was sweet to see Val's maternal instincts kick in on someone other than Gigi.

"Yay, girl movies!" Gigi took a sip of her piping hot coffee. As it burned down her throat, she wondered if the jet fuel might sear a hole in her stomach. Licking her lips, she sighed happily, not caring. The coffee would definitely wake her up. "Watching *Dirty Dancing* and *The Breakfast Club* won't annoy the crap out of Evan?"

"Nah, he's a girl dad. He's used to it," Val replied. "But we should probably mix in the original *Top Gun*, so he doesn't go completely crazy."

"Good idea. Also, I'd never complain about having to watch a young Tom Cruise saunter around on the screen."

"Same," Val agreed. "That's good for everyone. But besides movies, we'll also bake with Evan's mom, go ice skating on the lake, and have Sunday supper with the family. Plus, Issy is part of a Christmas art show at the high school. I might even get you on a horse."

"Gah, I can't wait!" Gigi exclaimed, stepping out of the coffee shop and into the crisp winter air. "We're going to have so much fun."

As she wrapped her scarf snugly around her neck, a genuine smile spread across her face. She was truly happy for her sister. Val had rekindled a romance with the kindest, sweetest man. Evan was perfect for her, and Gigi was thrilled they were back together. Plus, Evan's family was wonderful, and Gigi was excited to spend a week with them all.

It warmed Gigi's heart to see Val creating a family of her own, but a small part of her felt envious. She hated admitting it, but deep down, she longed for the love and stability Val and Evan had found. For so long, Gigi had prided herself on her independence, determined to navigate life on her own. But watching her sister settle down had shown her that a relationship could be stable and healthy—unlike the tumultuous ones she'd witnessed growing up.

"You said you're meeting Alice and Paige?" Val asked, breaking through Gigi's thoughts.

"Yeah, we're going to the farmer's market together." Gigi's boots crunched through a snowbank as she crossed the street, headed toward the train station where she'd hop a ride to the indoor market. "We like to be the first ones there, before it gets really busy." Even though she was tired, Gigi wasn't about to miss out on the Saturday morning ritual with her besties, especially since their Christmas pajama party got cut short last night.

"What're you shopping for?"

"Lots of stuff. Local honey, fresh ricotta, salami, and veggies. There's this lady that sells microgreens and I want to pick up garlic, onion, leek, and fennel to try in a few new recipes I've been experimenting with."

"New recipes? You're making me hungry. You know I love your cooking."

"I'll make them for you when I visit. I want your feedback." Gigi had also been playing with a business plan for the food delivery service she'd told Harris about. It was coming together, making her excited for a side hustle of her own. Maybe somewhere down the line it even could blossom into a full-time gig. But first, she'd need to save and plan. Hitting her bonus this year would be enough to get it started, and she was so close to making that happen.

"Getting on the train soon," Gigi said, picking up her pace as the caffeine set in. "But I can't wait to see you. I've got so much to tell you, Sis."

Chapter Twenty-One

Harris dropped the thick folder on his dad's desk. The slap of papers echoed in the massive corner office, which was ninety percent glass and leather. "Dean and I came up with a new proposal for the business together."

His dad stared at him from the opposite side of an obnoxiously wide desk. He leaned back in his chair, a skeptical look crossing his face. "So, you ended up revising your proposal? Why?"

"I changed my mind about SheTime. We need to invest in that side of the business. Dean agrees. There's so much untapped potential."

"Your last proposal recommended we dissolve SheTime." Wrinkles deepened and fanned out from his father's eyes. "Now you want to invest in it? What could have possibly changed that much in the last few weeks?"

Harris met his father's critical gaze, everything he'd experienced with Gigi flitting through his mind. "I made a mistake."

His dad's head veered back like he couldn't believe what he'd just heard. "A mistake with the numbers? That's not like you."

Harris shook his head. "No, I made a mistake by *only* focusing on the numbers." Harris paused, gathering his thoughts. His father's sharp eyes bored into him, waiting for an explanation. "I've been working closely with Gigi, and I don't think you understand how incredibly talented she is, and how much passion she has for the brand. She has endless ideas and a deep understanding of the market, but she's been operating with minimal resources. You've been running SheTime too lean, expecting her to do too much on her own."

His dad frowned, obviously not liking Harris's answer. "So, you're saying the lack of success is because of my underinvestment, not the product or market demand?"

"Yes. Exactly," Harris replied, steeling himself under his dad's scrutiny and powering on. "The products are amazing. Customers who use them love them. But we haven't given Gigi the tools she needs to grow the business. She needs a team under her, people who can help with social media, public relations, content creation, events. She needs a bigger marketing budget to reach a wider audience."

His dad shook his head, looking disgusted, which was not the reaction Harris was hoping for. "Are you serious?"

Harris nodded confidently, knowing he needed to go deeper, go back to what he believed in. "You asked what could have changed in a few weeks' time." He paused, amazed that one person could flip his opinion completely in such a short time. "Well, I've seen firsthand what Gigi can do with limited resources, and I'm confident she could grow that business tenfold with a proper team and funding. SheTime has the potential to not only survive but thrive and become a significant supplement to our larger business."

His dad stilled, as though the "tenfold" comment had finally grabbed hold of his cynicism and shook it. He cocked a brow. "Tenfold?"

"Yes," Harris confirmed.

His dad thrummed his fingers on his desk. "I'm listening."

"You've undervalued Gigi. Her instincts are excellent. She's incredibly creative and delivers results under pressure, with little to no resources. She's the one that has built SheTime from the ground up." Harris pointed to his proposal, a thrill shooting through him as he finally captured his dad's attention. "I was wrong to think that dissolving SheTime was the solution. We need to invest in it, support her, and give her the resources to succeed."

His dad's eyes narrowed, but Harris could tell he was considering the proposal. "You're betting a lot on one person, Harris. What makes you so confident she's worth it?"

Harris paused for a breath, picturing the passion in Gigi's eyes, the determination in every expression, her endless optimism. "Because she reminded me that success isn't just about numbers. It's about people. And I believe in her. I think if we give her the chance, she'll exceed our expectations. She's the one that needs to lead SheTime, not me."

The silence that followed fell hard on Harris's shoulders. His dad stared at him, dissecting his words, piece by piece. When he finally spoke, his tone was curt and simmering in doubt. "You've got everything laid out in here?" He tapped his pointer finger against the folder.

Harris gave a nod. "I do. Every detail."

His dad pursed his lips, looking sour. "I'll review your revised proposal, but I think you're speaking out of turn. Investing heavily in a niche business is a significant risk. I wasn't on board when Dean originally started SheTime, but I let him do his thing." He paused, festering in annoyance. "If I agree to this, there will be expectations."

Harris clenched his jaw, biting his tongue as his father referred to women's skin care as niche. It was a massive market. Yet, he knew that disagreeing with his father now would only agitate him further, make him double down on his opinions.

"Read the proposal," Harris replied. "I believe it's a risk worth taking."

Two days had dragged on like an eternity. Harris hadn't seen Gigi since the night they lost and found Rudy, and the void was palpable. She'd been busy setting up the last Gift Guide event, while Harris had been consumed in board meetings with his dad and

Dean, along with having video calls with his GambleOnLove team. A few exchanged emails, snarky signatures, and evening phone conversations did little to quench his longing for her.

Gigi really was like a drug. His mind eased and his spirit soared in her presence. His heart might burst if he had too much of her, yet he craved more. The need was beyond his control.

Navigating the bustling crowd on State Street, Harris scanned the sidewalk ahead, looking for Gigi. He smiled wide when he spotted her, standing near the entrance to Macy's, waving at him, looking as bright and shiny as the golden trumpets and sparkling garland that trimmed the historic building. His pulse quickened as he neared. A satiny skirt peeked out below her long peacoat. Her dark, velvety hair was down, curling into soft waves. Her eyes sparkled with excitement, and Harris yearned to wrap his arms around her, lift her off her feet, and kiss her as if no one else was around.

Reluctantly, he steeled his arms, resisting the urge.

"You look beautiful," Harris greeted her, reminding himself they were at a work event.

"Thanks." She practically twinkled. "You're looking extra dapper yourself." She tipped her head and a lock of hair fell across her cheek and neck. He dug his fingers into his palms, fighting the powerful urge to brush her hair back, to tuck it behind her ear.

"I can't wait to show you the window!" Gigi bounced on her toes, breaking up the battle Harris was having with himself.

"I can't wait to see it," he replied, anticipation building in his chest.

Tonight was long awaited, the largest and last of all the Gift Guide events. It was the grand finale. Besides the brunch, which would start shortly, each sponsoring business had decorated one of the famous Macy's window displays. Gigi had been planning and preparing her creation all year. She'd told him about the display but hadn't revealed the details of the design, keeping it a secret and a surprise for today.

"Close your eyes," Gigi said, taking hold of his arm. Harris buzzed with her touch. "Then I'll take you to our window."

"Close my eyes?" He quirked an inquisitive eyebrow.

"Yes," she insisted, smiling.

"Close my eyes and walk down an icy sidewalk packed with a million people?"

Gigi laughed at his resistance. "Yes! Do you think I'd let you fall?"

"Maybe?"

"Never," she replied through a grin.

"Okay. For you, I'll do it."

Gigi took his hand, and Harris shut his eyes, surrendering to her guidance. He followed her voice and touch, reveling in each sensation, all his senses on fire. Her warm, soft hand in his. The sweet vanilla fragrance she exuded. Her contagious laugh that Harris was sure he could pick out from seven states away.

Each step felt like a promise, a whispered secret shared between them. The world around them faded, leaving only the warmth of her hand and the thrill of the unknown.

"We're here." Gigi guided him to a stop, her voice brimming with excitement. "You can look now."

Harris opened his eyes, first finding Gigi's beautiful face. Then he blinked against dazzling lights, wondering if he'd stepped into a dream. The Macy's window showcased a Winter Wonderland—a snowcapped, enchanted forest, framed in gold. Fake snow twirled down from above, dusting emerald pine trees. Woven through branches, twinkling lights cast a magical glow, and woodland creatures danced through the trees.

In the center of the forest was a vintage clawfoot bathtub, overflowing with glittering ornaments. A cozy fireplace crackled in the background, its warmth almost palpable through the glass. Plush white towels and robes were draped elegantly over branches or pooled in the snow, inviting relaxation. And an array of SheTime soaps and lotions artfully adorned the scene, each product glowing under soft spotlights. A pedestal showcased one boxed gift set, elevating it like a precious artifact.

Harris gawked, taking it all in. Then he turned to Gigi, struggling to find words. He was speechless. *SPEECHLESS.*

"Do you like it?" she asked tentatively, her hand grasping his forearm.

His eyes were wide with admiration. "Gigi, this is incredible. I don't even have words. You've created something truly *magical.*"

Her eyes flashed with relief and then pride. "You really think so?"

"Absolutely. This . . . this is beyond what I imagined. How did you . . . how did you even do this?" He waved a hand at the scene, at the piece of art before them. He knew what kind of budget she'd worked with, yet she'd knocked this project clear out of the park.

She smiled brightly, nerves replaced with joy. "Lots of work. And negotiating. I managed some great deals. Found the bathtub at a garage sale. It has a hole in the bottom, but I didn't need it to hold water. It just needed some paint. The trees and animals came from a local high school. Bought them from the theater department after their spring run of *The Sound of Music*. I got all the lights and ornaments on clearance last year, the day after Christmas."

"Really?" he asked, dumbfounded.

She nodded. "You can accomplish a lot by getting up early, putting in some elbow grease, and having crafty friends."

Suddenly, it became clear to Harris why his father didn't give Gigi more support. She did it all without a single complaint. He was letting Gigi do the work of ten people, because it saved him the cost of a team.

"I hope you weren't doing this off the clock," Harris said, gathering that she had and wanting to give his dad a piece of his mind.

"It's fine." She shrugged. "Besides, how many people get to create a window display for Macy's? I wanted it to feel special, to really showcase SheTime. I tried to capture the way our products should make customers feel—like they are being whisked away to a luxurious fantasy, even in the midst of holiday chaos." Her smile widened.

Harris pushed down a flash of anger aimed at his dad, not wanting to rain on Gigi's parade. He'd deal with his father later. Right now, this moment was for Gigi.

Scanning the scene, he lingered on the intricate details. The effort, thought, and love Gigi had poured into this project was evident. "You've outdone yourself. This is beyond perfect."

She blushed. "I'm so glad you like it."

Gigi still had her hand on his forearm, and Harris set his hand on top of hers. He wanted to take hold of her, to kiss her and tell her how amazing she was and how much she meant to him, but he held back. "What are you doing tomorrow night?"

"On Christmas Eve?"

He nodded, losing himself in her dark-chestnut eyes.

"Having an early dinner with my nonna," she replied, looking confused. "Why?"

"After you celebrate with your nonna, would you join me for the Christmas Ball at the Ice Castle?" Never in Harris's life had he wanted to take anyone to a ball, but the emotions Gigi pulled out of him were different. He wanted to sweep her off her feet, make her feel like a queen every minute of every day. And he knew the Christmas Ball would be something Gigi would love.

Her red lips opened, as if he'd confessed he could fly. "Are you asking me on a date?"

Harris stepped closer, wanting his intentions to be clear. "Gigi, will you be my date for the Christmas Ball tomorrow night?"

"I—" The twinkle returned to her sweet eyes. "If I'm going to be your date for the ball . . . I might need to go dress shopping tonight."

Harris grinned. "I can coordinate that. Is that a yes?"

Gigi nodded, her head bobbing up and down excitedly. "Yes, I'd love that."

A wave of adrenaline washed through him, and Harris couldn't stop his impulse. His fingers gently lifted her chin, tilting her beautiful face up so he could dive straight into her eyes. He leaned in, the need to kiss her overpowering, but just as their lips were about to meet, a lurking figure behind Gigi caught his attention.

Glancing up, Harris froze when he discovered his father standing a few strides away, watching and judging.

Chapter Twenty-Two

Everything had been perfect—Harris's reaction to the window display, his invitation to the Christmas ball, the fireworks that had exploded in her chest when he leaned in for a kiss. But just when she expected his lips to brush hers, he'd pulled away. His dreamy gaze vanished, replaced with a seriousness that stilled her.

Harris stepped back, clearing his throat. "I'm sorry. I shouldn't have done that. This is a work event."

Gigi's brain malfunctioned, glitching like a broken computer. It took a few seconds to process the change in Harris, but she ultimately managed a nod. "Yes, of course." She forced a smile, despite the confusion swirling inside her.

Harris searched her gaze for a second longer, as if gauging her reaction. "The event's about to start. We should head inside."

"Don't want to be late," she replied, forcing robotic cheer.

As she mulled over what had just happened, Harris guided her through the crowd and into Macy's. He kept his hand on her lower back, which confused her even more. She couldn't deny he was right. They shouldn't be kissing at a work event, but what had stopped him at the last moment? Did he regret asking her on a date? Had the reality of them together suddenly jumped up and slapped him in the face? Or was he simply trying to be responsible?

Inside, the store was full of last-minute shoppers. The buzz of chatter and Christmas music surrounded them. It was no place to instigate a serious conversation with Harris. Instead, she bit her tongue and followed him into an elevator. They ended up on opposite sides, packed in like sardines, but Gigi still had a direct line of sight to Harris. He looked like a statue—stoney and sullen. Was he even blinking? He avoided eye contact with her completely, and by the time they reached the seventh floor, Gigi was as tightly wound as spooled thread.

Once off the elevator, they moved past displays of candy and chocolates, stopping under the arched entrance to The Walnut Room, the department store's historic restaurant, where the brunch would take place. Harris turned to her, and Gigi hoped he'd address the sudden change in his demeanor. Instead, he went straight to work talk.

"Do you need any help with the product display?" he asked.

She shook her head. The floor below her heels felt unsteady. "No, it's all taken care of."

"Okay, I'm going to head in for brunch then. I'll see you afterwards, right?"

"Sure," she replied, not sure what he truly meant. He'd see her later, after work, when he could go back to the man she was falling in love with?

Harris gave her a flat, unconvincing smile before walking away. As he disappeared into the restaurant, Gigi couldn't help acknowledging their stark differences. Harris wasn't just her boss. He was a man from a world of wealth and privilege. He was joining his family, to mingle with board members and other business owners, likely to sip champagne and nibble appetizers. Meanwhile, she'd be working, representing his family's company. The disparity between their lives seemed to widen with each step he took from her.

With a sigh, Gigi turned away. Could they honestly make a go of this? Was she out of her mind, thinking they could blossom into real life? Was she only entertaining Harris until he went back to New York?

Wanting to stop the tornado of doubt, Gigi headed into The Walnut Room, toward the retail area in the center, which was set up around the base of the restaurant's towering, iconic Christmas tree. The forty-five-foot tree nearly touched the ceiling of the two-story space. White lights, glittering ornaments, and silky white-and-gold ribbon adorned it. The base was trimmed with life-size nutcrackers and shiny presents. Usually, it took Gigi's breath away, but at the moment, she couldn't appreciate its beauty.

Plastering on a smile, she weaved through product displays, finding the table she'd set up with SheTime's Christmas Collection. She tidied it, angling every box just right. Then she chatted with the other vendors, trying to immerse herself in the festive spirit. But her mind kept deceiving her, drifting back to Harris. She couldn't help glancing around the restaurant and into the crowd, unsuccessfully looking for Harris amongst the white linen tables and dark-wood paneling.

Was he thinking of her too?

Thankfully, shoppers quickly filed in, distracting Gigi. She got swept into greeting customers, helping them select products, and pointing them toward the registers. Minutes stretched into an hour, and when there was a slight lull, Gigi went to find a Macy's associate. The gift sets were selling quickly, and she'd need more brought in, but as she wound her way to the front of the restaurant, a familiar voice caught her attention. She stopped in her tracks and quickly discovered the source. Just a stone's throw away, Harris and his father were talking. They stood in the hallway off the main entrance. Harris's back was to her. His tone was low, and Mr. Ryan's expression could've peeled paint from the wall.

Startled, she took a step back, hiding behind a column. She was just about to backtrack when she caught a snippet of their exchange.

"... your proposal to dissolve SheTime," Harris's father said, his voice filled with determination and finality. "I agree with it. It's the right answer. The numbers just don't support keeping the division going."

Gigi's breath hitched. Her heart stopped. What were they talking about? Dissolving SheTime?

Numbly, Gigi stepped closer to the edge of the column, her ears straining to hear more.

"Did you read my entire proposal?" Harris replied, his tone tight. "I don't think—"

"Yes, I read the entire thing," his father interrupted. "We can't keep sinking money into a failing venture. It's better to cut our losses now."

A chill grabbed Gigi's spine. Harris wanted to dissolve SheTime? Her breath increased as their conversation sunk in. Had Harris wanted this all along? What did that mean for her job? For her future? Harris was kissing her and holding her and telling her she was so wonderful . . . and at the same time, he was planning to fire her?

Harris spoke again, but his tone was so low that Gigi couldn't make it out. However, she clearly caught his father's response.

"SheTime isn't viable," his father almost growled. "It's not personal. It's business. You know that. Or, at least, you should know that."

Tears stung Gigi's eyes. Her heart pounded in her ears. She couldn't believe what she'd just heard. Unable to bear another word, she plowed forward, wanting to get out of the restaurant as quickly as possible. She hoped to God Harris didn't see her because she couldn't face him. Not now. She wouldn't believe a word he'd say. The man she was falling for didn't think she was capable, didn't think the business she'd built was worth saving, and that hurt more than she could've imagined.

Fleeing the restaurant and jogging into the store, Gigi zigzagged around shoppers, heading for the elevators. Her vision blurred as she ran, disappointment and heartache deceiving her, pushing tears over her lashes. And her heart leapt to her throat when she heard her name.

Harris was behind her, calling to her.

Please, let an elevator be open. I just want to leave. Never in her life had she run out on a job or a commitment, but she couldn't look him in the face. She just needed to be away . . . by herself, to process.

"Gigi!" he called again as she neared the elevators, finding them all closed.

"Come on," she groaned, pushing the call button multiple times, but not one elevator obliged her plea. When Harris rushed around the corner, she squeezed her eyes shut, telling herself she wouldn't cry in front of him.

"Gigi, wait," Harris said, and she wiped her eyes with her fingers. When he put a hand on her arm, she yanked it from him, and he had the nerve to look hurt.

"Why would you lie to me?" she asked, questioning every gut instinct she had. Harris was not the man she thought he was. How could she have looked past his red flags? Why did her heart blind her so? Did she have some weird fetish for men that would break her heart? "You're going to dissolve SheTime?"

Color drained from his face. "It's not what you think—"

"What is it, then? Because I think you've been playing with my emotions while planning to eliminate my job."

"I haven't—" Harris stopped himself, taking a breath as if he were the one in the tough spot. "I haven't been playing with your emotions."

She immediately noticed he didn't reference her job. "But you *have* been planning to fire me?"

"No, I—" He tossed a hand through his hair. "What you must've overheard . . . it's not the whole truth."

She peered at him, scanning his face, not sure why he looked conflicted. "What's the truth, then?"

His features steeled, but his eyes somehow stayed soft. "I did propose to dissolve SheTime," he admitted, and Gigi's mouth fell open. "Before I met you. Before we worked together." His jaw squared, and Gigi questioned the flex of muscle. "The first thing I did when I got to Chicago was a financial analysis. I went through the numbers. I thought I was being efficient, that I'd help streamline the business before I went back to my life in New York."

She shook her head like she might rattle some sense into it. Eventually. "And you decided it would be best to get rid of SheTime?"

"I did," he breathed. "But then I started working with you, and you changed my mind. You helped me understand the potential of the business. You proved me wrong, and I've been fighting for SheTime ever since."

Gigi's mind swirled, ruminating on his words. Raw emotion shot through her. "But your father said—" A lump hit her throat, cutting off her words.

Harris shook his head, looking torn. "My father was upset because he saw us together, in front of your window, when I was just about to kiss you."

"What?" Her stomach roiled, crashing like a wave. Could anything else possibly go wrong?

"I'll handle him. Please don't worry. He's only upset because of the proposal—"

"I can't." The words slipped out of her mouth, stopping Harris mid-sentence.

"Gigi, I—"

She reached out, putting her hand on Harris's chest, stilling him. "I don't know what to think. I need time. Space." Her heart was heavy, pulling her down. She wanted to go somewhere quiet, to process what had happened and all the sharp emotions cutting through her.

Harris's mouth parted, looking defeated by her response. But instead of fighting her, he quietly said, "I understand. Take all the time you need. Just know that I'm here when you're ready to talk."

Just then, an elevator finally opened. Gigi dropped her hand to her side. She couldn't bring herself to say another word. She took a step back and turned, leaving Harris for the empty elevator. But as the doors closed, she caught the longing in Harris's eyes. Instantly, her heart clenched, and her stupid instincts told her to throw a hand out to stop the door. Instead, she fisted her fingers, keeping them from making another reckless mistake.

Chapter Twenty-Three

The elevator door shut, sealing Gigi away from Harris, and a profound emptiness settled over him. He'd known the risk of telling her the truth about SheTime, but he hadn't expected the gut-wrenching reality of her pulling away. For a moment, he considered going after her, running down seven flights of stairs to head her off on the first floor. He wanted to say something, anything, to make her stay and hear him out. But she said she needed space.

He had to respect that, even if it tore at him.

Gutted, Harris turned and walked back into the restaurant. The dining room was a numbing hum of holiday cheer, with families and friends gathered around tables, their laughter mingling with clinking silverware and glasses. The Christmas tree in the center of the restaurant glittered with ornaments and lights, a stark contrast to the darkness he felt inside.

His father had already taken his seat at their reserved table and was engaged in a lively conversation with a couple of board members. Watching him go about his business as though nothing had just happened made Harris's blood boil. Did he get high from getting his way? From manipulating everyone around him? At his breaking point, Harris decided he'd had enough.

As he approached the table, his father looked up, his expression shifting to one of mild curiosity. "Did you get that handled?" he asked, his tone laced with disapproval.

"What would you like me to handle?" Harris replied, forcing his voice to remain steady and clear, projecting down the long table for every board member to hear. "The fact that you've underpaid and undervalued one of our best employees? That you've limited SheTime's growth because of your own stubbornness? That you're essentially blackmailing your own sons to get your way?"

His father leaned back in his chair, looking shocked at the accusations, but Harris stood firm at the head of the table. Every board member turned their head, giving Harris their full attention. Dean shifted in his seat, looking ready to stand up and jump into the conversation, but Harris didn't want him to be the peacemaker. Their father needed to hear what Harris had to say. He'd crossed so many lines and Harris wouldn't let him continue to, for both Gigi's and Dean's sakes.

"You're completely out of line," his father replied sternly. "This is what happens when your personal life interferes with business. You need to think with your head, not your heart."

Harris clenched his jaw, struggling to keep his temper in check. He would not let his father commandeer the conversation or disrespect Gigi. Besides, his father didn't have a leg to stand on. He'd demolished all his relationships, always putting work first. He didn't know what it was like to think with his heart.

"First of all, my personal life is none of your business," Harris started. "Those decisions are mine to make, and I don't need your input. Second, you can't understand a business by solely focusing on numbers and spreadsheets. You need to understand and support the people behind the business. That's what has the most potential to affect the numbers. You have a very creative and passionate marketing director and team, yet you haven't given them the tools or support for real growth."

"Are you serious?" His father scoffed. "Passion and creativity don't pay the bills, Harris. You know that."

"No, I don't know that," Harris replied. "That's what I'm trying to tell you. If you actually supported your team, gave them room to grow, the numbers would follow. Instead, you want to control every single decision. Why won't you consider or support thoughts and plans that aren't your own?"

His father's expression hardened. "You've been back here for a month and think you know everything, don't you?"

Harris stared at his father, determination brewing inside him. "I don't know everything, but I know Gigi could step into the director role with SheTime and easily double the business in a year. She could grow it tenfold in a few years, given the right support. I also know that Dean doesn't need my help to take over Ryan & Ryan. He's got more passion and experience with the family business in his pinky toe than I ever have. And if you'd get out of his way, he could actually apply his own ideas, which are fresh and new and also have the potential to greatly increase sales."

His father glanced from Harris to Dean and back again, and Harris challenged him with a stare. If he opened his mouth and lashed out at Dean next, Harris was certain he'd snap. Every protective instinct was on high alert.

"But if you read through my entire revised proposal, you'd know all of this already," Harris pressed his dad. "Did you share the revised version with the board?"

The board members exchanged curious glances and his father's face flushed red. His mouth tightened into a thin line, but he kept silent. It was all the answer Harris needed. He knew his father well enough to know he'd hashed through every detail Harris had lined out. It was likely why he'd been so triggered when he saw Harris and Gigi together. He'd been wound up by Harris calling him out, and latched onto the first thing he could hold over Harris's head.

"I don't think—" his father started, but Dean stood abruptly, cutting him off.

"I'll send it out for the board to review," Dean said, looking down the table at Harris, grit and admiration in his eyes. "I agree with every point Harris laid out in the revised proposal, except one." Harris guessed what Dean was about to say. There was only one angle they couldn't agree on—that Harris would step away from Ryan & Ryan. "I want to run the business *with* Harris. I think we're better together, and despite the way our father brought Harris back, I am grateful to have had this past month together. And I hope I can convince Harris to stay."

The brothers shared a look that hit Harris in the chest. In a strange, twisted way, their father's manipulations had brought Harris and Dean closer. He could see himself staying and working alongside his brother. Yet Harris had little confidence that their father would ever relinquish control of the business, even after retiring. Moreover, Harris's feelings for Gigi were growing stronger every day, and he wanted a future with her. They couldn't sustain a professional and personal relationship, and he knew which of those he wanted to continue.

Giving Dean an acknowledging nod and a strained smile, he addressed the table. "Please review the proposal and let Dean and Mr. Ryan know what you think." The board members nodded, some more enthusiastically than others, but Harris knew he'd made his point. Without waiting for a response from his father, Harris stepped back from the table. "Excuse me. I've got something very important to address."

Turning and walking away, a sense of resolve hardened within him. He wouldn't let his father's narrow-mindedness dictate his actions. He had to fight for what he believed in, for what he knew was right.

And most importantly, he had to make things right with Gigi.

Chapter Twenty-Four

Gigi spent the rest of the day in her apartment by herself. She didn't tell a soul what happened, mainly because she still couldn't believe it. The deception hadn't fully set in. Was her internal compass broken when it came to love? Did it mistakenly tell her she was going north when she was actually pointed south? Grabbing a few more tissues, she slumped into her comfy armchair near the window, blowing her nose and wiping her eyes.

Sighing, she tilted her head back, setting it against the backrest. She looked up at the beige ceiling, analyzing what had happened. She'd stupidly fallen for her boss, and he'd deceived her in the worst way possible. He'd captured her heart and was eliminating her job . . . taking her independence and livelihood. Dumbfounded, her gaze slid to the window. She followed a trickle of snowflakes as she tried to understand how she'd let her life fall apart.

Was she the most naïve woman in the world? She'd thought they had something special, that Harris cared about her. She'd been dreaming of what their life could look like together. But instead of finding her happily ever after, she was sitting in her apartment, alone. Not even a cat to keep her company. Then Gigi thought of Rudy, and that sent her into another fit of tears.

She sniffled, wiping her nose and telling herself to buck up.

You have amazing friends. You have a wonderful nonna and sister. You are strong. You'll be fine, no matter what. You'll figure it out. You always do.

She repeated her thoughts, trying to soothe her heartache and worries, knowing she had a wonderful life and a solid support system. Yet, there was still something inside her that wanted Harris, that yearned for a partner to share her life with.

Just as she cursed that part of her, her phone dinged, stopping her heart. Gigi stared at the phone on the windowsill, not sure she wanted to see who was texting or what they had to say.

"If I pick you up and the text is from the phone company, thanking me for paying my bill, I'm going to throw you across the room," she threatened the inanimate object.

A few breaths later, she gave in and reached for her phone, finding a text from Harris.

I want to give you space, but I also need you to know exactly what happened. I was wrong. I proposed to dissolve SheTime before I knew what I was talking about. But I promise you I fully believe in the business. I believe in you. You made that business, and you are the only one that can take it to the next level.

Please check your email. I sent you the proposal I made when I first got to Chicago. And I sent you my revised proposal. I want you to see them for yourself and make your own conclusions.

Then, if you want to talk to me afterward, please let me know when I can see you. Because I have a lot more to say, but I will only say the rest in person.

Sincerely & truly sorry for my boneheaded mistake,

Harris

Hurt, confusion, and the craziest bit of hope battled inside Gigi as she sat there, staring at her phone. She read his text again. And again. She considered throwing her phone across the room, but her arm wouldn't follow through with it. And the longer she sat with his words, the more conflicted she got.

Blowing out a breath from the bottom of her lungs, Gigi dropped her phone to her lap. She remembered the pain and longing on his face as the elevator doors closed; how he'd run after her. Could reading the proposals help her understand his decisions? At the very least, it might give her some closure and understanding of her next steps.

Closing her eyes, Gigi breathed in and out, preparing herself for what she was about to do. Then she went to the kitchen and pulled her laptop from her tote bag, where she'd discarded it on the table. Sitting back down in the armchair, she covered herself with a blanket and opened her computer on her lap.

She fired up Outlook and saw Harris's email at the top of her inbox. When she clicked it open, there were no words, just two attachments. The first document was titled "Before Gigi." The second was "After Gigi."

Chapter Twenty-Five

Gigi had stayed up far too late, reading through the proposals Harris had sent her. The first proposal, titled "Before Gigi," was brutally cold and calculating. He'd outlined a plan to dissolve SheTime, citing underperformance and recommending layoffs, including Gigi's termination. Pain and embarrassment pierced her when she saw her name reduced to a mere line item. The clinical language was harsh and blunt. Yet, as she examined the numbers and information Harris had, she could understand the conclusions he'd drawn.

She still couldn't believe he'd recommended cutting an entire division, like it was a plant that wouldn't flower. Instead of trying to understand why it wasn't thriving, he wanted to pull it up by the roots and be done with it.

But when she read through his revised proposal, "After Gigi," the difference was stark. He'd stressed SheTime's potential, advising an increased marketing budget and dedicated team. But what shocked her the most was his suggestion of promoting her to Director, with back pay for being underpaid in her current position. In his summary, Harris said she could double the business in a year, if given the right support.

The revised proposal was not written by someone that saw her as expendable. Someone who believed in her wrote it. Even as she thought of it now, sitting in her Nonna's apartment, overwhelmed tears filled her eyes.

"Gigi, mia bella, come make your plate. Dinner is ready," her nonna's sweet voice broke through Gigi's thoughts, urging her to stand from the floral couch. After a slow morning, Gigi had gone down two floors, to her nonna's apartment, trying her best to put on a happy face. After all, it was Christmas Eve, and they were spending the day together. Gigi cherished these moments and didn't want them ruined by the dumpster fire that had taken over her mind.

But she hadn't fooled her grandma. From the second Gigi arrived, Nonna knew something was wrong. When Gigi said she wasn't ready to talk about it, Nonna started cooking.

Gigi joined Nonna at the kitchen counter, where she was cutting into her baked gnocchi with the edge of a serving spoon. Bacon, spinach, tomato, and mascarpone cheese were laced through the casserole. The aroma of garlic, basil, and rich tomato filled the apartment, offering comfort in the form of a grandmother's love.

"Thank you," Gigi said, holding a plate while her nonna filled it. "This looks absolutely delicious."

Nonna smiled, loading up the second plate. "Sit, eat. Let's enjoy."

Gigi carried both their plates to the table, setting them between silverware and tall, cold glasses of milk. Gigi sank into a chair and reached for her nonna's hand. They bowed their heads and said a thankful prayer, as they did before each meal.

Taking her first bite, Gigi moaned in appreciation, thinking her nonna was right again. Food made everything better, especially homemade gnocchi and warm, gooey mascarpone cheese. "This is incredible," she said, licking sauce from her bottom lip.

"I'm glad you like it," Nonna replied, but she was quiet for a few beats, and Gigi felt her eyes boring into the side of her head. When Gigi looked up, Nonna asked, "Are you ready to tell me what's troubling you?"

Gigi swallowed hard. She wasn't ready, but also wondered if her nonna had sprinkled truth serum over the gnocchi—because the entire story spilled out. The night they lost and found Rudy. How Harris had kissed her and confessed he was falling for her. His plan to dissolve SheTime, and the revised proposal she'd just read.

Her nonna listened intently, nodding occasionally. When Gigi finished, she took her hand. The warm touch prompting Gigi to share more.

"I'm just—" Gigi confessed, resting her forehead in her other hand. "I'm so confused."

Her nonna squeezed her fingers, keeping hold until Gigi turned her head to look at her. "Mia bella, I'm going to tell you something I learned over forty years of marriage. It may not be what you want to hear, but it may also save you a lot of heartache."

Gigi stared at her, not sure what to expect but trusting her nonna completely. She nodded, wondering if her nonna would tell her to cut Harris off and run the other way. Could she ever look at him again if that was the advice?

"Love is not always easy. People make mistakes, sometimes big ones," Nonna started, surprising Gigi. "No one is perfect, and forgiveness is an important part of marriage. It's an important part of any relationship."

Gigi pressed her lips together, taking in this piece of advice. "But how do I know if I can trust him again?" Her voice sounded small, unsure, thinking of the part of the revised proposal where Harris had expressed his desire to step away from Ryan & Ryan. Was he already on the next flight, back to his life in New York? The thought of permanently losing him sent Gigi into a tailspin, despite what she'd learned in the past twenty-four hours.

"If there's genuine remorse and a willingness to change, it's worth considering forgiveness." Nonna offered a consoling smile, as if she could see the conflicting emotions pouring through Gigi. "Trust is built with time and effort. It sounds like Harris realized his mistake and is trying to make amends. If he's willing to fight for you, then maybe he deserves a chance to explain himself."

Gigi swallowed, wanting to believe Harris cared for her, that he wanted to be with her. But could she risk demolishing her heart by putting it on the line one more time? Before she could respond, there was a knock at the door. Gigi looked up, puzzled. "Who's that?" Someone was stopping by on Christmas Eve?

"I'm not sure." Nonna started to rise from her chair, but Gigi stood quickly.

"I'll get it. You finish your dinner." Gigi strode to the door, opening it to reveal Paige's and Alice's smiling faces. They stood in the hallway, each with garment bags slung over their shoulders.

"What're you doing here?" Gigi asked, her surprise clear, even though she was excited to see them. Paige and Alice exchanged a glance before stepping inside.

"We have a mission," Paige announced. "To get you ready for the Christmas Ball."

"What?" Gigi asked, spinning to watch her friends march through the apartment. They slung the garment bags over the back of the couch.

"Holy moly, those are heavy," Paige said, rubbing a shoulder.

Alice grinned at her, before they each hugged Nonna, offering Christmas greetings.

"Did you say something about a ball?" Nonna asked, and Alice nodded.

"Harris came to my bookstore just before closing last night," Alice started, pure excitement on her face. "He begged for me and Paige to help, saying he really messed up, and that he needed to make it up to you, and he wanted to do it in person."

Nonna raised a wise brow. "He said that, did he?"

Alice bobbled her head at Nonna. "He asked if Paige and I could deliver a letter to you." Alice raised her hand, and Gigi zoned in on an envelope, her heart skipping a few beats. "And four ball gowns." She waved at the garment bags like she was Vanna White.

"Do you have any idea how hard it is to get ballgowns on the eve of Christmas Eve?" Paige raised her brow before her expression softened. "He must really have it bad for you."

Gigi's heart was now pounding. She didn't know what to think.

"Do you want to read it?" Alice asked, offering the letter.

"Please," Paige added. "I'm dying to hear what it says. I wanted to read it on the way over here, but Alice wouldn't let me."

Alice smirked. "I had to wrestle it away from her." She held the envelope out in front of her, as if she'd stumbled on Santa's naughty or nice list.

Gigi tentatively took it from her. As she opened the envelope and unfolded the letter, her hands trembled. In the quiet that followed, Gigi absorbed the neat, black cursive on cream paper.

Dear Gigi,

I couldn't bear to put any more words into an email or a text. I had to at least put pen to paper to try to convince you to meet with me.

What I really need to say must be done in person. I know you're upset, and you have every right to be. I should've been upfront with you, telling you what I'd proposed to my father. I hate that you discovered that when you overheard our conversation. It should've come from my mouth.

If you read through the proposals I sent you, you can see that I changed my mind about SheTime. You did that. You showed me all the potential I couldn't see in spreadsheets and charts. I hope you know I meant every single word I said to you. I know how amazing you are, what a catch you are for any man or any company.

But what I really need to say to you has nothing to do with business. Your lovely friends obliged me by delivering my message, and a selection of dresses for you to choose from.

Will you meet me at the Christmas Ball? Please hear me out. I'll be waiting to see your beautiful face at seven o'clock at the fountain. I've enclosed your ticket.

Sincerely, truly, madly, deeply . . . falling for you,

Harris

Gigi peeked inside the envelope, finding a ticket to the ball. She looked up at her friends and Nonna, too stunned for words. All three of them were leaning forward, like they might hear her thoughts as she'd read the letter.

"Well, what'd he say?" Alice said, eyes wide as saucers.

"I just about died while you read that!" Paige's mouth was open. "*Please*, don't make us wait a second longer!"

Nonna sat at the table, her hands pressed together in anticipation. "Mia Bella, what did the letter say?"

Gigi glanced back at Harris's penmanship, at every swoop and dot that he'd penned for her. And Nonna's advice echoed in her ear—forgiveness is an important part of love.

Maybe it was time to stop letting her fears dictate her decisions. Maybe it was time to follow her heart, instead of run from it. Deep down, she wanted Harris in her life, which meant she had to trust herself enough to take a chance. Hearing Harris out could be that chance.

She looked up again. "He wants me to meet him at the ball."

Chapter Twenty-Six

Harris stood in the courtyard, staring at the grand fountain, which was chiseled from ice. He focused on the swirl and carve of each wave, the smooth of molded dolphins, all while trying to wrangle his anxiety. In the towering ice castle behind him, the Christmas Ball was in full swing. Music and laughter filtered out through the arched, open entrance, but the only thing Harris cared about was seeing Gigi's beautiful face.

With a deep breath, he blew out his worries, letting them steam through the frosty night air. What if she didn't come? What if he'd irrevocably screwed up the best relationship he'd ever had?

Anticipation stabbed him in the gut. Since Gigi left him staring aimlessly at the closed elevator, Harris couldn't stop thinking of her and every special moment they'd shared. The way she smiled at him, the warmth of her touch, the joy in her eyes. He couldn't listen to a Christmas song or eat a single bite of food without wondering what she was doing, or if she might forgive him.

Tonight was his chance to make things right, to tell her everything he'd been feeling, to convince her to give him a second chance. But as the minutes ticked by, Harris's heart sank further and further. Maybe she wasn't coming after all. Maybe she'd read his letter and tossed it in the trash. Maybe he'd blown it.

Turning from the fountain, he scanned the courtyard again, chastising himself for not going to her apartment in person, for banking on the fact that she'd show up at his request. Shaking his head in disappointment, Harris's gut twisted at the idea of losing her forever. But then, out of the corner of his eye, he caught movement. He turned and his breath caught in his throat.

Gigi walked through the entrance to the courtyard, looking like a Christmas miracle. She'd chosen the red velvet gown with the billowing skirt, and seeing it on her now, Harris couldn't imagine a more perfect choice. A white faux fur shawl covered her shoulders, and her hair fell in loose curls, framing her face and classic beauty. Under the moonlight and stars, she looked like an angel.

Harris started toward her, trying to steady his breathing and steps, to calm the pounding of his heart. When he finally reached her, he offered his hand. Her warm, soft touch glided into his, and Harris's stomach scattered to pieces.

"Gigi, you look stunning. Absolutely breathtaking," he whispered, knowing he couldn't describe with words how beautiful she was. "Thank you for meeting me tonight."

A soft smile touched her red lips. "I wanted to hear what you had to say."

Harris took a breath, his emotions swirling within him like a snowstorm. "Gigi, I need you to know I truly appreciate your brilliance and passion. I can't say that enough. I believe in you, in everything you can achieve, with anything you set your mind to." Harris searched her eyes for signs of hope. "Did you read both proposals I sent you?"

She nodded. "I did."

"I wanted you to see for yourself what I laid out for my father. I need to make it known beyond any doubt that you alone changed my mind about SheTime. You deserve to run that division, and we should support you with a budget and team that matches your talent. I truly hope my father sees the light and does just that."

"I appreciate you saying that," she said, before pressing her lips together, looking like she was grinding over what he'd said. "But I realized something very important while I was reading through your proposal."

His heart slowed to a stop. "What's that?"

"I expected to be recognized without ever really asserting my worth."

Harris tilted his head, listening intently. "What do you mean?"

Gigi took a deep breath, gathering her thoughts. "Reading your proposal made me realize that I've been waiting for someone else to validate my contributions. I've been playing it safe, hoping Kim or Dean or Mr. Ryan would notice my value and reward me for it. But I can't rely on others to fight my battles for me. And that includes you." Her gaze was steady and determined. "I appreciate your support. I really do. But I reached out to Mr. Ryan and told him I need an appointment right after I'm back from Christmas vacation. I'm going to ask for the director position myself, along with the salary I know I deserve. It needs to come from my mouth, Harris. I want it to."

Harris felt a rush of admiration for the woman standing before him, looking every bit the queen she was. "Gigi, that's incredible. I'm so proud of you for making that decision, and for asking for what you want. You deserve that and so much more."

"I have some questions for you too."

"I want to give you answers."

She stepped closer, her hand tightening around his, and he wanted to pull her into his chest. "Are you leaving Ryan & Ryan? Going back to New York?"

"I'm leaving the family business," Harris confirmed, and his heart jerked as Gigi's face fell. "Dad and I had a talk late last night. I told him we need to work on our relationship instead of the business. Until we can iron out our differences, it's best to keep work and family separate. He actually agreed and said he'd move forward with handing the business over to Dean."

Gigi sighed, her eyes crinkling in sadness. "I'm happy for Dean, but I was hoping you'd stay."

Harris's breath hitched, grateful for the small omission of her feelings. He took both Gigi's hands in his. "I want to stay . . . *for you*. Not for the business."

Her eyes widened, hope pushing out sadness. "What?"

"That's what I wanted to ask you in person." He cleared his throat. "If I stayed in Chicago, would you consider dating me? Would I have a chance of calling you mine?"

Her mouth fell open, but she was quiet, and Harris continued, wanting to make sure she knew what he felt for her. "I made arrangements to manage GambleOnLove remotely. I'll have to go back after the holidays to get some new processes set up, but Adam and I built a strong team, and they can handle the day-to-day operations. That's one more thing you taught me—that I need to trust my team. Ironically, I need to take my own gamble on love. And I want to do that with you."

Her lips tilted up into the most beautiful smile. "Are you saying you want to take a gamble on me?"

"I'm saying I started falling in love with you the day you tackled me on the elevator, and now I can't picture my life without you in it."

She squeezed his hands, her eyes twinkling. "You couldn't resist my Christmas kitten sweater?"

"I couldn't resist the person who'd wear such a sweater." He grinned at her, his heart pounding. "Gigi, you're bright from the inside out. You bring joy into every situation. I can't imagine one more day without you. I sincerely and truly am in love with you.

Please, give me a chance to prove it to you every day, every moment from here on forward. I love you, Gigi."

Her eyes glistened, and she clutched his hands like she might fall over. He held tight.

"Harris, I . . ." She paused, and Harris nearly collapsed with anticipation. "I love you too," she blurted, like she'd been holding that secret.

Harris sighed and laughed in the same breath, an immense relief washing through him. Nearly floating, he closed the distance between them and cupped her face gently in his hands. "Thank you," he began, joy radiating from his heart, "for making this the best Christmas ever."

Gigi leaned in, her smile radiant. "Best. Christmas. *Ever*," she echoed softly.

Their lips met in a tender, heartfelt kiss under the moonlight and stars. Wrapped in each other's embrace in front of the magical ice castle, the world around them seemed to blur, leaving only the two of them in their own fairytale.

At that moment, Harris knew that this holiday season would be unforgettable. It would be one to remember, for all the right reasons.

Epilogue

NEW YEAR'S EVE

Gigi stood facing Harris in his living room, under the string of lights still twinkling over the window. Remnants of lasagna, Caesar salad, and champagne were scattered across the island in the adjoining kitchen, where Paige and Alice were chatting with Nonna. Everyone was happily digesting the beautiful meal they'd cooked and enjoyed together.

"I can't believe you found someone who could fix this," Harris said, staring down at his mother's Christmas ornament. The snow globe sat in the palm of his hand, sparkling as the glitter inside the dome swirled.

"You can find anything in the city if you look hard enough." Gigi squeezed his arm and smiled, delighted at Harris's excitement. "You should've seen the guy's shop. There were floor-to-ceiling shelves filled with old clocks, toys, music boxes, basically anything with a tiny motor. Plus, he honestly looked like Santa Claus. He might've had elves in the back room."

Harris grinned at her suggestion. "I really hope he did."

"Go ahead. Wind it up."

"It's been forever since I've heard this play music," he started, turning the tiny gold crank on the bottom of the globe. As the first few notes played, Gigi couldn't stop her smile from consuming her entire face. When she'd picked up the ornament, she'd turned the crank herself. She already knew what song it would play.

"Is that—" Harris looked at her in disbelief.

"Mariah Carey!" she yelped, jumping at the same time.

"No way!" Alice shouted from the kitchen, as the signature notes of "All I Want for Christmas is You" chimed through the air.

"Yes, way!" Gigi replied, now dancing. Alice, Paige, and Nonna joined, raising their champagne glasses as they swayed.

Harris laughed, pulling Gigi into a big hug. "Thank you," he murmured into her hair. "This is really special."

"I'm glad you like it." She leaned into him, squeezing him back.

"I love it and I love you," he murmured, his voice filled with affection.

"Love you too." She smiled into his chest, and he swayed them into a little two-step. Gigi pulled back just enough to look up at him. "I knew you secretly loved this song."

"It brings back all the best memories." He grinned, brushing a strand of hair from her face.

Gigi giggled, remembering a stewing Harris standing on stage in a crazy reindeer sweater, shaking jingle bells, and wishing he was anywhere but there. That might've been the moment she'd truly started falling for him. "For me too."

Harris kissed her on the forehead and Gigi closed her eyes, taking in the moment, until Rudy went zipping through the living room, bouncing off furniture like he was auditioning to be one of Santa's flying reindeer.

"Rudolph!" Gigi called out his full name as he somersaulted across the couch, tumbling with one of the knit toys Alice had made him. Everyone laughed at the kitten's antics, and Gigi scooped him up, snuggling him into her arms. "You better behave for Nonna."

"Oh, he'll be sweet as pie for me. Won't you, my little sugar plum? We're going to have the best time," Nonna said, walking over from the kitchen to scratch Rudy on the head. He closed his eyes in delight. "Speaking of, you guys better get going if you're going to make your way to the Pier."

"Thanks for hanging out with Rudy tonight, Nonna," Harris said, giving her a one-armed hug around the shoulders. "Since this is our first New Year's together, I'm not sure how he handles fireworks, and I'd be a mess worried about him all night."

"Of course," Nonna replied, tossing her hand like it was nothing. "You young'uns have a great time. I'm beyond excited to snuggle up with Rudy and watch the countdown from the couch.

We'll be tucked in the guest room bed before you give Mia Bella her New Year's kiss."

"Nonna," Gigi said, with a blush. "Who said I'm kissing him at midnight?" She winked at Harris.

"She'll make me work for it." Harris winked back, sending a ripple of tingles through Gigi's belly.

"All the good ones do," Nonna replied, chuckling, and Gigi beamed. She adored how her nonna had immediately taken to Harris.

After Gigi had arrived back in Chicago after her wonderful visit with Val, her nonna had insisted on having Harris over for dinner. Over rigatoni, they'd instantly hit it off, and when he'd surprised Gigi by telling her he wanted to adopt Rudy officially, that had sealed the deal. The news had pushed Gigi to tears, and her nonna had squeaked something in Italian. When Gigi asked her what she'd said, Nonna explained it translated closest to, "he's a keeper."

"Enjoy, my sweets! Happy New Year!" Nonna waved as Gigi, Harris, Alice, and Paige filtered outside, excited for the evening to come.

They walked down the bustling streets, the city alive with anticipation. When they reached the Navy Pier, hopeful possibilities of a new year filled the crisp air. The four of them located a spot near the Ferris wheel that offered a perfect view of the fireworks. While enjoying peppermint hot cocoa, endless chatter, and laughter, Gigi felt an overwhelming sense of gratitude for her beloved family and friends. In the end, that was all that really mattered—who she shared life with.

With just a minute to spare until midnight, Gigi raised her cup. "To another year filled with laughter, love, and unforgettable adventures! Cheers!"

"And an extra cheer to the new director of SheTime." Harris beamed at Gigi, and her insides melted. "Congratulations!" Paige and Alice followed with congratulations of their own.

"Cheers!" they all said together, clinking their drinks, and when the countdown began, they shouted together.

"Three! . . . Two! . . . One!"

The sky erupted in a dazzling display of color and lights. Shouts of "Happy New Year!" filled the air. The promise of a new start shot through the crowd.

Harris turned to Gigi, his eyes reflecting the fireworks as he pulled her close. "Happy New Year, Gigi," he whispered, leaning in.

"Happy New Year, Harris." She closed the distance between them, wrapping her arms around his neck. "You can kiss me now."

He smiled and did just that, blinding her with fireworks of their own.

Thank You

Thank you for reading *Sincerely Not Yours*! I hope Gigi & Harris's love story touched your heart the way it touched mine. If you enjoyed it, I'd love it if you would post your honest review anywhere you purchased your book. Reviews help me understand what stories readers enjoy. They also help me decide what to write next. Your review is greatly appreciated! And if you loved it, tell your friends! The best way to spread the word about a book is through word of mouth!

Never miss a new release ~ Join Brittney Joy's newsletter:
http://www.brittneyjoybooks.com/newsletter

Maple Bay Series

WOULD YOU LIKE TO VISIT MAPLE BAY?

A sweet small town romance series with heaps of heart—where family dinner is a must, and someone will always leave the light on for you.

Checkout the Maple Bay Series here:
https://www.brittneyjoybooks.com/maple-bay

Also by Brittney Joy

Sweet Romance Books:
Rescued in Maple Bay
Starting Over in Maple Bay
Second Chance in Maple Bay
Country Stars in Maple Bay
Matched in Maple Bay
Christmas in Silver Leaf Falls
Sincerely Not Yours

Red Rock Ranch Series: Young Adult Contemporary
Lucy's Chance
Showdown
Rodeo Daze

The OverRuled Series: Young Adult Fantasy
OverRuled

OverRun

OverThrown

Checkout all books here:

www.brittneyjoybooks.com

About the Author

Brittney Joy writes sweet stories full of hope, heart, and happily-ever-afters. She and her family live in their own piece of heaven in the Oregon countryside. They stay busy with their menagerie of silly horses, cackling chickens, wooly sheep, two very naughty goats, a scheming cat, and an adorable dog. When Brittney isn't writing, she's riding or reading. And she wishes she could do all three at the same time.

www.brittneyjoybooks.com